the every boy

the every boy

Dana Adam Shapiro

HOUGHTON MIFFLIN COMPANY

Boston | New York

2005

For information about permission to reproduce selections
from this book, write to Permissions, Houghton Mifflin Company,
215 Park Avenue South, New York, New York 10003.

Visit our Web site: www.houghtonmifflinbooks.com.

Library of Congress Cataloging-in-Publication Data

Shapiro, Dana Adam.
The Every boy / Dana Adam Shapiro.
p.   cm.
ISBN 0-618-47800-0
1. Teenage boys—Death—Fiction. 2. Diaries—Authorship—
Fiction. 3. Loss (Psychology)—Fiction. 4. Fathers and sons—Fiction.
5. Separated people—Fiction. 6. New York (N.Y.)—Fiction.
7. New England—Fiction. 8. Grief—Fiction. I. Title.

PS3619.H3559E94 2005
813'.6—dc22 2004065135

Book design by Melissa Lotfy

Printed in the United States of America

QUM 10 9 8 7 6 5 4 3 2 1

For Mimi and Grammy

the every boy

1

For his fifth birthday Henry got two presents that would come to shape his soul. From Dad, a bean-stuffed cow that went *moo* when squeezed. Henry called it Moo. From Mom he got an inner voice, a grand and booming yes man for each of his stooped shoulders. Gift-wrapped in silver, *Great Ovations* was a forty-five-minute record filled with nothing but applause from "major moments" of the twentieth century. There was no context for the claps — it could have been a Puccini encore, Willie Mays on the fly in center field, hails for the Führer in Berlin. What difference did it make? The message never muddled, and while Dad thought it was coddling and hollow and bad for a growing boy's spine, Henry fell asleep to it every night for three years. He even carried a dubbed cassette in his knapsack just in case he needed exaltation on the go.

Dad found this out just before Henry's funeral, when he was first presented with the ledger his son had secretly kept since he was ten on over 2,600 sheets of loose-leaf graph paper. (Only girls kept diaries, Henry had been told.) Color-coded to reflect the author's changing moods, it was a catalog of life's wee tics and pangs, a tally of passed-down preferences for mustard, painkillers, snow blowers; how-to notes on taming a cowlick, skinning a deer, snapping a headlock, cleaning a toboggan. There were threadbare confessionals, overheard dialogue transcriptions, stabs at investigative journalism, and finally, on the last page, three maxims under the acronym AMFAS (As My Father Always Said).

1. Hit 'em back twice, three times as hard.
2. Burn me once, shame on you. Burn me twice, shame on me.
3. Don't wear red trousers to battle.

Why? thought Henry's father, his fifteen-year-old son in a box before him. He hadn't heard from Henry since he ran away four months ago, but it was becoming clear that the boy took little pleasure in his father's principles. Dad felt the pulse beats quicken in his wrists, a vein rippled up in his forehead. The mourners sat as he stood still and sweaty, the ledger on the lectern. He opened to a random page and started reading.

Page 2018: color-coded pink for "facts, ma'am"

9/9/88

My father's name is Harlan. He's very photogenic. A terrific winker. People say he has movie star teeth. On his fortieth birthday he had them whitened. "Like a picket fence," said Mom. He was coaxed into becoming a dermatologist in his late twenties. Truth is, he never had any real interest in medicine or humanity, but out of respect for community status he agreed to let his parents put him through medical school. Now he's pretty rich, but cheap. Loves to get the display model. Hates to valet the car.

Harlan couldn't stop reading. On page 2450, color-coded red for "world-changing," he first saw the name of Benna.

At Canal Street I think of Benna. How she'd crouch up in a ball and face the white-brick wall of our bedroom, my fingers between her teeth. How, one time, she opened up the window and pointed to a star: "That's how far away I feel from you right now."

She liked to pee at the same time as me, that is, with her sitting on the toilet and me standing up, facing her, aiming carefully at the small triangle of water between her legs. Sometimes she'd lick my stomach and try to make me miss. She called me "Roo" (as in kanga-), and I called her "Joey" because she said she liked to be carried around in my pouch. "Roo, I miss your pouch," she sometimes said over the phone.

Harlan wiped his forehead with his tie, the pale blue silk turning navy from the sweat. The crowd cramped up, uneasy. He had forgotten all about them. He flipped quickly through the ledger in search of an exit quote—anything to get off that stage. He paused on page 2610, color-coded white for "?," logged on March 20, 1989, the day before a shell painter found the soggy body washed up on the shore of Tenean Beach. Harlan spoke softly, trancelike, as if he didn't understand English.

Telling the truth is so much easier. Every lie requires a lifetime of maintenance.

The old man froze. He looked toward the ceiling, suspicious, as if about to get spit on. The guests turned pink. It was as if they'd been pulled into a private war, violent and looming. You could hear the heartbeats and then finally a sigh. Mom cued the record. The needle hit home, the temple filling with a century of reverence. *Those goddamn clapping hands*, thought Harlan. *I should've cracked them long ago.*

He did, in fact, one Scotchy day when Henry was at school. He took the record out back and launched it like a skeet. It shattered on the third shot from a bolt-action rifle, but the guilt came quick and heavy, and Henry's father found himself driving in and out of lanes to the record store. He even roughed up the jacket, scratched the vinyl where it had been scratched before so Henry wouldn't get any ideas.

But over the next few weeks, alone in the house with the ledger, the old man learned that Henry knew all along. About that and everything else.

2

Henry's patterns formed early, the result, according to his pediatrician, of an excessive enthusiasm spurred by feelings of displacement. "Nothing to bang your heads about," Henry would say, imitating the doctor, "just something to keep a thumb on."

Henry's father licked his right thumb filing coupons from the Sunday paper. But Mom kept both of hers on her boy. She knew him better: what he longed for, what he'd run from. His mouth still full of baby teeth, he'd case the girls in class, sneak up close, part their hair from behind like a curtain, and kiss them on the back of their necks. He had a thing for ears, too: pulling them, folding them, sticking paper clips or pencil erasers into the crooked holes—not hard enough to rupture any drums, but his shins were often purple from retaliation. Once he caught a pudding in the jaw from an ESL girl who had asked him repeatedly and politely in broken English to please stop sniffing her mittens. They were clipped to her sleeves.

"He earns his wounds," said Mom. "He needs the lessons, and sometimes the ice packs." In third grade he got two stitches in his eyebrow for refusing to un-jinx a loudmouth, who then silently whacked him with a branch. The following year, things turned ideological. Henry came to school on Martin Luther King Jr. Day wearing blackface and a noose, sitting in the back of the classroom and refusing to drink from the "white" fountain. That spring, roused by a history lesson, he insisted on carrying a warning bell as a sign of camaraderie with Old World lepers. "We're all in this together!" he cried, pumping his little fist. He was punished, of course, banished from recess, left with the lunch lady while the other children climbed tractor tires and played with sand. And as usual he was unrepentant to the death, lying head-down in the hall-way, his lips sealed with masking tape, his thumbs wrapped tight with fishing twine. The tape and twine were his idea.

At home he played the dutiful son, always on hand with a coaster or a dustpan or a "love you." He did as he was told. He'd surf his father's back for hours, riding the worn-in muscles with bare heels and toes, making faces at the back of his head. Dad wouldn't say a word, but when he'd had enough he'd roll out quickly so Henry would fall. "Wipeout!" Dad would yell, and they'd have a laugh—the father's genuine, the son's forced. It was something of a bonding device from a man who'd likely punch your arm for saying a fruity word like *bond*. Though ineffective, Henry appreciated the effort, once even upping the gag by flailing on the carpet, paddling to keep his head above water, scanning the reef for sharks. From the safety of the sofa, Dad offered his arm: "Grab the log, boy!" he yelled, his fingers stick-straight and tense. Their hands clasped and Henry was dragged ashore, his lungs gone salty from the sea. It was one of the few times they touched. Except for the boxing.

They never fought in the daylight, always after dinner. Dad would sit on the edge of his bed, defending himself with head bobs and open palms. Henry stood before him, shirtless and skinny in striped nylon trunks, puffy gloves laced up at the wrists, mouth guard in place, and a resting stool marking his corner. His hair was brushed back tight with Dep, his skin all Vaseliney so the landed blows would slip. On one side there was the older, self-crowned champion—the Enforcer. The challenger, being obsessed with dinosaurs and outer space at the time, fought as Stega Tunguska, named after the vegetarian roof lizard and the town in Siberia where the brightest meteor ever reported had crashed in 1908.

"Come up under the jaw," coached the Enforcer, slapping his son on the cheeks, butting his forehead with the ball of his hand. "The nose'll getchya blood—you can *shock* 'em. But the chin'll put 'em down." And he'd stick out his chin, taunting Stega with the target, his teeth going *clack-clack-clack*.

"Right," said Stega, hopping about, shaking off the pain. He didn't enjoy these times together, and he hated more than anything when Dad clacked his teeth. But like the surfing expeditions, he played along. He always thought it better to play along. Until the eve of his first double-digit birthday.

Then, in the fall of '83, just after his favorite meal of lamb chops, mint jelly, and strawberry-topped cheesecake, the perennial challenger came out swinging, ready to dent the Enforcer's record, if not his face. He went for the jaw, but as usual, his jabs were blocked flat, his hooks stopped midair. The Enforcer landed a crushing slap to the belly. Finally, as the round dwindled down, Stega narrowed his eyes, wound up big, head-faked left, and threw his weight behind his waist.

He cocked his leg, licked his lips, and *kapowed* the old man right where he wasn't expecting it.

Stega's eyes flashed pay dirt. "It is *not* looking good for the Enforcer," he announced, the champion spread out on the carpet, cupping his balls. "A-one and a-two and a-three," he counted, mixing jazz time with sportspeak, whistling at himself, strutting through the bedroom, gloves held high in the air. The Enforcer knew the victory, a first for Stega, would please him, but was taken aback when, upon trying to stand, he was kicked repeatedly in the ribs, hard, the final boot landing right under the chin: *Clack!*

"I'm sorry for unloading and kicking you where it counts," began Henry's six-page apology, written later that night in perfect cursive on the monogrammed stationery Mom had had printed for him at birth. Hardly a man of letters, Dad stopped reading halfway through the second page. "It was a good shot," he reasoned. "Strategic." Still limping, he took Stega out for a no-hard-feelings birthday brunch the following day. For dessert, they had a preordered ice cream cake in the shape of a boxing glove.

Mom didn't approve, said it was "like living in a cave with monkey-folk," and retreated to her beloved ant farms.

"Don't be strange," said Dad, following her into the bug room.

"To punch is strange," she said, annoyed, looking into her wooden, matrix-style terrarium. "To punch your boy is strange."

"He punches me, too! We punch each other!"

"He hates ice cream cakes."

A Scandinavian beauty with toplofty hair, Henry's mom assured him she would always be the same—backward and forward, from here to forever. Her name was H-A-N-N-A-H, she showed him on paper. Or M-O-M. She ran a successful party-planning business, mostly afterwork functions and the occasional wedding, bar mitzvah, or sweet sixteen. Her insights on the anatomy of a place setting or the thread count of a dust ruffle were unmatched in their suburban community, nine miles west of Boston. She was a bantam, bread-baking woman, artful and doting, neurotic enough to wash a peeled banana, and would unintentionally add fresh twists to old sayings: "It's on the top of my tongue!" Henry adored her.

When he was little, she'd stay late in his room, drawing pictures of him as he slept. She had fat pads filled with closeup sketches of his growing muscles, hands, and teeth, roughly rendered in black ink and charcoal. She wasn't trained or ambitious when it came to art; she was simply fascinated by her creation — not the drawings, the person. "This is mine," she'd say, checking Henry's pulse, looking into his nostrils. "This is me." She once counted his eyelashes with a magnifying glass and drew each one to scale.

Like her, Henry was prone to nosebleeds, occasionally waking with a crimson crust around his mouth and chin, his cheek stuck to the pillow. In the middle of the night Mom would feel a tap on her shoulder as Henry stood over her in the dark. The first time she screamed. Dad jumped up and fell back to sleep. Mom and son went downstairs to the bathroom.

"Why do I keep being bloody?" asked the six-year-old, sitting cross-legged in pajamas on the lid of a closed toilet.

"You have a big heart," said Mom, dabbing his face with a warm cloth. "Big heart, more blood."

"Really?" said Henry, touching his chest.

She spoke with an ambiguous accent, the result of growing up in a trilingual home, but her sentences always made sense. "Oh, yes," she said, touching his shoulder blades. "Sometimes I see it coming out your back."

Mom's first marriage, to an aspiring chef, ended fortuitously two weeks after their rotten honeymoon. She was at the market, buying all his favorite ingredients, thinking about how to tell him she'd made a big mistake. He was at the house, fiddling with the rain gutter, and looked up too late to see an air conditioner falling from the attic window. Out of respect, the missus wept well and cursed the constellations, but she'd secretly wished upon those very stars. The mister, she'd said, was a cheapskate, with mean bones in his body and day-old meat in his fingernails. Her mourning was swift, the tombstone top-notch, and three weeks later Hannah met Harlan outside a flea market in Oak Bluffs, Massachusetts.

3

In the fall of '83, just after Henry turned ten, Mom packed her fundamentals and set out for yet another fresh start, in the Netherlands. "Just a breather," she assured Henry. "For the greater good of the family."

The couple had gone from seeming bliss (six months) to nearly happy (two years) to quiet misunderstanding (seven years). There was no open warfare, no last straw—it was the status quo that killed it. She was off now to grow tulips and raise weaver ants in Haarlem, the famed flower district by the North Sea. For her dearest, she left the sketchpads and a double batch of his favorite cinnamon buns. "I love you so much more than everything," she said, crying, realizing in that moment that Henry's patterns came from her. "I'll write every week. Every week until I return."

For her husband she left the following note, stuck to the refrigerator with a heart-shaped magnet:

I forgive you.

In her absence Henry's father searched for answers and meaning. He sold his gainful dermatology practice and set out in search of sizable hobbies. The first was weapon collecting, an interest that was sparked after watching a film on Henry Derringer and peaked with a magazine feature on machete-wielding teens in West Africa. At its most eclectic, his cache included a Belgian cane gun, an original Parsons Knuckle Knife, a pair of lead-lined leather gloves, a homemade zip gun, an eighteenth-century blunderbuss, and a jaguar bar return, which is a device that looks like a bat with razor blades for wings.

The collection stopped growing when Henry stumbled onto it, donned the lead-lined gloves, and started punching everything in sight. He broke three knuckles on his right hand and two lamps in the living room. *It could have been a lot worse*, thought Dad, and he took the medical bill as a warning. After that came a more innocuous, pell-mell pursuit of animal lore, the ex-doctor taking great pleasure in flanking his phrases with weirdo bits of history and science. *In sixteenth-century Peking, one recipe for revenge entailed mixing ground-up tiger's whiskers into an enemy's food; in 1386, a French executioner publicly hanged a hog for mangling a little girl; Virgil once spent 800,000 sesterces (about $100,000) on a funeral for a housefly . . .*

But mostly Henry's father chased his boyhood enchantment with jellyfish, still finding it fascinating that these deadly, passive drifters have no brains. A dinner story he often told Henry was based on the short life of a prominent Frenchman who, for his thirtieth birthday, received an all-expenses-paid snorkeling vacation to the west coast of Australia. Just before brunch, the man took a dip, and while doing a lazy version of the elementary backstroke, bumped into an Irukandji jellyfish about the size of a shaved baby carrot. The man kept swimming, thinking little of the encounter. Half an hour later, the venom kicked in. Sharp cramps spread through his body, followed by respiratory failure and lesions on his face, neck, and forearms. The pain, according to Henry's father, was equal to a thousand dog bites, and then came the coma, and ultimately death. Following the incident, the resort was abuzz with *Jaws*-like tales of tiny monsters, and while no official alarm was sounded and the beaches at the resort remained open, guests were encouraged to swim in the pool.

It was on page 769 of the ledger that Harlan saw this story reprinted almost verbatim, color-coded gray for "shady." This put him in a foul mood, as the details, to the best of his knowledge, were true. He refused to touch the ledger for seventy-two hours. It was tough to stay away — it was all he had left of his family — but he respected his own authority. When he returned, he landed on that name again, Benna, written big and bold, again and again and again.

Page 1170: color-coded clear for "glee"

11/25/88

I meet her in line at a food stand: she orders a hot dog with everything, hold the hot dog. Then she looks at me and says, "With all that stuff on there you can't even tell it's missing." She offers me a bite and wipes my mouth with a napkin after I take it. "Good," she says, blinking, clean around the eyes. She chews her food casually, like it's a piece of gum. I ask for her name; she tells me. She lives at the Alcazar, she says, a hotel on Fifth Avenue.

For the next twenty-four hours we don't leave the room. We open the curtains periodically, but never for more than twenty minutes at a time. We drink hot chocolate with marshmallows and lie around on extra pillows that are brought to the door with shiny green mints. No matter how many times we ask for more pillows, they are delivered promptly and with a smile. (We collected almost three dozen: some foam, some feather.) Wearing robes, we make fresh tea and watch the water change from clear to auburn. She pokes the tea bag with a pen and the leaves leak everywhere. We order fruit shakes and waffles and champagne. We have a staring contest. A thumb war. We look our names up in the phone book. We build an igloo out of pillows and pretend to freeze to death.

"I liked it when you caught me singing in the shower," she said in the morning, without lipstick, without a bra. We were lying on the bed with the lights on, friends who'd known each other only a short while. Some time in the night we just started kissing. We each took off our own pants. "Underwear on," she said. In the morning I woke up with my cheek pressed against her stomach, her fingers in my hair, and Benna all over everything.

4

Eighth grade was a turning point, the year in which Henry came to fathom puffy themes like fate and purpose, and the prickly difference between the *good* and the *greater good*. He took music lessons, showed promise, and dropped four instruments from the woodwind family. And he had his first sexual crest by way of an old friend — his beloved, faithful Moo.

One night he couldn't sleep and started rub-rub-rubbing. It felt good, then better, then *boom*. It was a dry run, but powerful, and despite a feeling he described in his ledger as "mythical," it filled his growing head with trouble. He wasn't sure what had happened, if something had burst or been mended, and the possibility of the former was driving him wacky. He was anxious during the day, in a swivet at night, needing to go back but too scared to go. In his ledger he wrote of the antediluvian days, before all this: a more gullible, loose-toothed, pyromaniacal time when black widows and king cobras were bloodthirsty beasts, when stuffed cows were pals, and sex — even a handjob — was as far-fetched and grandiose as jet packs or pots of gold.

But those days had passed, he knew. And while he thought

his father could shed some sense on the transition, he knew better than to seek his counsel. He had learned early on that you keep the really big things to yourself, and this, he had a hunch, might be one of those things.

He would, however, make exceptions for Jorden, his new best friend, a green-eyed, pigtailed girl two months and two inches his senior. She'd recently moved to town from Vidalia, Georgia. When they convened at the bike rack for one of their sessions, she looked flat-faced and moody, like she needed the time for herself. They assumed their position: she sitting on the grass, leaning against the bars, he with his head in her lap. Jorden wanted to be a psychoanalyst when she grew up and Henry always thought it best for her to get a jump-start on the dynamic. But this time he felt awkward—it was this very position that had inspired the rubbing in the first place.

Jorden rearranged his hair and explained that the concentration pills were helping, but that she hadn't written a decent diagnosis since taking them.

"It's hard now," she said. "I go to the park and all I think about is nature. In school, I think about school."

"That means it's working," he said. "You're too ready for it."

"I'm not," she said, fiddling with his earlobe. "I'm not ready at all."

Henry tapped his front tooth with his thumbnail. He tapped when he was nervous.

"Does your dad like baseball?" she asked.

"He likes hockey better."

"Is he compulsive? Like, does he get emotional about it?"

"He eats microwave popcorn while he watches. It gets all over the floor. Sometimes he wipes butter on the walls."

Henry shrugged. "I don't know if he really likes it, though. I think he just *likes* to like it. He's very into jellyfish now. Probably because my mom left and she's real into ants."

"I think I'll be a baseball fan," she said. "That'll be my sport to root for. Better than hockey, better than car racing."

"Better," he said.

"Are you gonna choose a sport?"

Henry ripped bunches of blades from the lawn. He was very worried about getting an erection. "Who kills themselves more, boys or girls?"

"Boys," said Jorden, unfazed by the topic switch.

"You know for a fact?"

"Girls try more, but boys are better at it. Suburban teenage boys are best. Suicide is very suburban."

"What's the youngest kid to do it?"

"Seven, I think."

"Girl?"

"Boy."

They'd known each other for just about a month, but each day Henry grew more proud of her. "How'd he do it?"

"Pills," she said. "Like, eighty. Antidepressants."

"Where'd he get them?"

"From his doctor," she said. "He was depressed."

They sat for a while, in position, her hands on his head, his hands on the lawn. Henry puffed out his cheeks and let the air seep through his lips. Neither of them wore a watch, but they could tell by the sky that it was almost dinnertime.

Jorden covered his eyes: "Twenty years from now, we could still eat meals together, right? You and me, no matter what?"

Henry smiled and put his hands on top of hers. "We could watch baseball while we eat."

* * *

That night Henry's father threw pork on the grill, baked pota-toes in the toaster oven, and chopped the lettuce into salad. He preferred iceberg, and so did the boy. "Anyone says differ-ent is selling buffalo," said Dad, unpretentious to a fault, backing up his wisdom with a wink.

"Except for Mom," said Henry, defending her preference for romaine.

The old man gave the nod — a quick bounce of the head, his bottom lip pushed up and out as if to say *you got me*. Henry knew that Mom had scratched his worldview something awful. He'd never admit it, but you could see it in his nods.

"Set the plates," said Dad, and Henry did: a napkin, fork, and steak knife placed on dishes on opposite sides of the round table. Each man was responsible for his own drinks and condiments.

The meal stayed on track: napkins on the laps, elbows off the table, the diners trading occasional Q's and A's between bites, nothing personal, nothing mean. Henry had impecca-ble manners (Mom's doing), and Dad abided as well, though it was an effort. Sometimes he'd slip and Henry would call him on it: "Knife be*hind* the fork." It was a showy thing to do, but Henry got a rise out of it, and it made him feel closer to Mom.

After dinner, they tidied up. Henry was the washer, Dad cleared and dried. When they were done, Henry caught a playful rat-tail on the arm. The dishrag was wet and it stung, a pink welt pushing through his shoulder. He winced and shook his head.

"What?" Dad frowned, tossing the rag in the sink and messing up Henry's hair.

Henry pulled away, rubbing the wound.

Dad grabbed the sugar bowl and turned on the stove. It

was electric and fired up immediately. "See this here?" He took a pinch of sugar and held it high above the heat. A flurry fell from his fingers onto the coil, orange now and scalding. The crystals popped into tight little fireballs. Henry's eyes popped as well.

"Do it again," he said.

Dad did it again. The room filled with a yummy redolence, sweet, like cotton candy or toasted marshmallows. Henry reached for the bowl, but Dad said, "Uh-uh." Then he took down the cinnamon, kept in a jar that Mom made—one of the last of her plain-sight relics. He took a pinch, held it high, and sprinkled. Very different, the cinnamon. Laid out on the coil, the grains glowed soft like spectral dust, then faded slow, the smell more aromatic, spicier than before.

"Which did you prefer?" asked Dad. "Which would you rather be?"

Henry took a chance. "Sugar."

"Wrong."

"How do you know?"

The old man stared at him. They looked nothing alike. Dad was boxy, Henry like a razor. Dad had blue eyes, Henry, brown. Dad had fallen arches; his hair was blond and wavy, long in the back. Henry's hair was darker, straight, his hands and feet like supple skeletons. They were both hardheaded with prominent ears, but Dad was softer in the cheeks, heavier in the jaw, with a close-cropped mustache he tweezed like an eyebrow. Henry planned on having a bushy beard as soon as he was able.

"Or—" said Dad, grabbing Henry, sliding an easy half nelson under his arm, around his neck.

"Cut it out!" yelled Henry.

Dad gave one of his nods. He pulled a scissors from a

drawer, quickly clipped a wisp of Henry's hair, and let him go. He dropped the hairs on the stove. They singed and melted, smelling up the room.

"Don't be a hair," said Dad. And he walked away, shutting off the lights.

Henry stood there in the dark, staring at the orange, quieting the urge to burn the place down. He grabbed the scissors, stroked the blades. He cut some hair off the back, an attempt to further distinguish himself from his father. He cut some more, tossed it on the stove. Within minutes he looked more like an AWOL private, his hair a fetid nest of smoke.

The detector went off. Big footsteps on the stairs. Henry placed the scissors on the coil and bolted, quick as he could, out the stinking door and down the street, zigzagging as if to throw off the snipers.

As expected, Jorden was sleeping when Henry arrived at her front door. She always conked out after big meals.

"Every, m'boy!" said her dad, plump as an alderman, standing on the farmer's porch, eating an ice cream sandwich and blowing bubbles through a plastic wand. "She's napping."

It was just the two of them now. The outdoorsy type, Jorden's mom had been part of a hiking troop. In the winter of 1982, on a tour through the coniferous forests of Canada, she was knocked dead by a drunken moose. The beast had been feasting on rotten fermented apples, turned aggressive, and from behind a tree came charging at the poor woman. The troop bore her name in memory.

"Napping?" said Henry, out of breath from the run over. "I can wake her."

"What's with the hair?"

Henry rubbed his head. He hadn't seen it yet, so he simply

shrugged. Jorden's dad nodded. He always knew when to leave a shrug alone.

A geology professor at a local community college, Jorden's dad was the "gather 'round" type, a *mind* man, but not lofty. He was a lifelong lover of rocks; you'd make his day by asking about the pliability of pure gold, say, or the difference between stalagmites and stalactites. *The former is basically an inversion of the latter; one's a drip, the other a pile. Pure gold's about as soft as Silly Putty.* "And he'd give it to you straight like that," wrote Henry in his ledger. "Real easy, not like other smarty types who make their brains seem all orphic and hallowed. He really *enjoyed* his smartness. He was always up to make you a personalized list of great books or records. Not the ones that experts liked, but ones that *you* would like. He was right, too, most of the time."

"Pick a sport yet?" he asked, stirring the soapy water.

"Can't decide," said Henry.

"Track and field, good variety there."

"Running? Yuck."

"Ever throw a javelin?"

"We threw shot puts in gym."

"I could see you throwing a javelin."

"Jorden picked baseball," said Henry. "She thinks it's romantic."

"How's that?"

"The songs," said Henry, eyeing the bubble bottle. "And the grand slams. She thinks grand slams are the greatest."

Jorden's dad noticed Henry's eyes and offered him the wand and bubbles. Henry accepted. He dipped and blew a thin stream, then asked, "Mind if I throw a twig at her window?"

"If you can reach."

"Sure, I've done it . . ." He paused, not sure if he'd said too much.

"How 'bout from there?" Jorden's dad pointed beyond the steps, a good ten feet away. He looked through the shrubbery and found a long, lean stick.

"Try it with this," he said. "Over the shoulder, long and soaring."

Henry took the stick and walked beyond the steps. He turned and hurled it, long and soaring, hitting his target square on the pane. Jorden's dad said, "Olympic," and Henry smiled, believing him.

"Hey!" Jorden lifted the screen and stuck her head out the window. She had a terrific capacity for waking up, no lag whatsoever.

"Come down!" said Henry.

"Morning, Skidoo!" Her dad, big into sobriquets, took the name from an old movie. Henry was always simply "Every, m'boy!"—exclamation point included—on account of his last name being Every.

"I'm not sure I should," said Jorden, coughing. "Dad, do people still get whooping cough?"

"You don't have whooping cough," he said flatly.

Jorden had of late been studying long-gone diseases and their vaccinations. She had devoted hours to rubella, diphtheria, lockjaw, measles, mumps, and polio, and was now apparently onto whooping cough (or pertussis), which she'd learned could be fatal, particularly in infants younger than six months. She wasn't a hypochondriac—it was more of a quest for proof that things could get better. Not anything specific, just a general, all-purpose betterment.

Accepting the prognosis, she closed her window and came

out to the porch, walking into a swarm of soapy bubbles. Her dad kissed her forehead, told Henry to work on his toss, and said he'd be inside should they need him. It was just before nine.

"How can I help you, Every, m'boy!?" said Jorden, borrowing her dad's inflection.

"What's whooping cough?"

"Bacterium," she said. "Coughing fits."

Henry stood back, protecting his nose and mouth.

"Don't worry, they fixed it. What's up?"

"I was wanting to ask you earlier." He put down the wand. "You know my cow, the one that *moos* when you squeeze it?"

Jorden listened with calm concern, a real pro. Henry, of course, did not apprise her of her inspirational role in the matter. When he finished, she said, "I see" and brought him into the library. From the top shelf she retrieved a book, first published in the mid-1800s, called *Dr. E. B. Foote's Plain Home Talk: A Cyclopedia of Popular Medical and Social Science*. She consulted the table of contents, opened to the chapter called "A Destructive Habit," and handed the book to Henry. He began aloud, then quickly switched to silence, his lips moving as he read:

Masturbation, or self-pollution, is prevalent among both children and youth. Five in every ten over twelve years of age bear the marks of this disgusting vice, although the evil is not so prevalent with girls as with boys.

To show how enslaved a child may sometimes become to the habit, and how unable to relinquish it after its health-destroying consequences are discovered, a most appalling story may be related about a young man. He consulted me at about the age of nineteen years, after he had become entirely impotent. At a very early age he commenced the habit of masturbation, and at fourteen, by some means, became aware of its injurious effects. He tried repeatedly to abandon the habit, but resolution was weakened by the effects the vice had produced upon his mind, and after many attempts, and as many failures, he actually tried to castrate himself with a jackknife. He succeeded in removing one of the testicles, but nearly bleeding to death, and fearing to make a confidant of anyone, he desisted from completing the operation, and his habit continued to enslave him till he became impotent physically and wretched mentally.

Jorden was taking notes on Henry's facial expressions: amusement, worry, fear. She was about to tell him the sundry details of a doctor-performed gonadectomy, but he gulped and asked, "May I borrow this?"

"Of course," she said. But knowing her friend, and that the book included chapters such as "Amorous Dreams," "Nymphomania," and "Seminal Weakness," she should have been more careful. Obsession, she knew, was Henry's folly. He inherited a total fear of fowl from his grandmother Lulu, who as a child was locked in a closet with a wicked pigeon (the bird got stuck in her hair). After hearing the story, Henry ate neither chicken nor egg, preferred Porky to Daffy, and abstained from all games of duck-duck-goose. He spent weeks circulating antipigeon propaganda and dropping seed laced with spermicide through the local streets and parks. And out of reverence for what he loved most, he would never refer to girls as *chicks*.

The first of his amorous dreams was eight years his senior, a C.I.T. at summer camp. She never wore a bikini, always this black and white one-piece that Henry thought looked like a navy vessel. He imagined her charging topless through seas with whole crews on her back—telescopes, flagpoles, swords—ducking waves like a porpoise, shooting water out her spout. He secretly longed for her murder, not out of any ill will, but because the idea of avenging his dearest was appealing—as a career, as a way of life. He wanted to love his work.

The house was too quiet when Henry returned, the old, gray book tucked into his pants like a pistol. Dad always fell asleep with the TV on, but there was no sound coming from his room. Henry walked into the kitchen. The smell of burnt hair still lingered, but everything was spotless, the scissors back in the drawer.

"Dad? Dad?"

He checked the living room, de-decorated since Mom left, then the den, the basement. He worried that maybe Dad had burned his hand and rushed himself to the hospital. If anyone would put the scissors away after getting burned it was his father. He was always yelling about putting things back where they belong.

Henry opened the refrigerator and took a chug from the chocolate bottle before heading upstairs. The steps always creaked, but tonight they seemed creakier. He flicked on the hall light. "Dad?" The door to his room was open. "Dad!" *If he went to the hospital he'd need some essentials*, thought Henry, and he checked his sock drawer, his medicine cabinet. But everything was where it belonged.

Walking out, he noticed the door to his own room was closed. His door was never closed, unless he was in there. He stared at the knob, confused, then walked downstairs to get a knife, just in case. He still believed in monsters, and that monsters could be killed with knives. But holding the weapon scared him even more, and he put it back. He fumbled through the drawer and grabbed an eggbeater.

Feeling a little silly, he returned to the door and knocked. There was no answer. He put his ear to the wood and could have sworn he heard a window closing. Finally, he took a deep breath, turned the knob, and led with his shoulder, still sore from the rat-tail.

Henry jumped. The eggbeater clanged on the carpet. In the middle of the floor, surrounded by candles, lay Henry's special cow, freshly shorn and spread out on a pillow, its face wrapped in cellophane, its hooves bound with shoelaces. The perpetrator left no note, but Henry had a pretty good idea. A monster, indeed.

5

Page 2366: color-coded blue for "philosophical"

2/4/89

It's dark now, and cold, but I still prefer winter to summer. Summer is by far the most boring of the seasons. Spring turns to summer and so what? There's hardly a change, you barely even notice except to complain that it was much nicer before. But summer to fall, fall to winter, winter to spring — these are transformations. To me, anyway.

Today I walked around the downtown area. SoHo, Tribeca, the path along the Hudson. Much better than the suburbs. People's priorities, I mean. In the suburbs everyone's all fussy about exteriors: their homes, their cars. Our next-door neighbors have hand-painted garbage cans. I like it better in the city. There are no garbage cans to paint, no driveways to decorate. Everyone drives the same car. In the suburbs, nobody really knows anybody but everyone knows who everyone else *is*. Or so they think. The city, it seems, is much more honestly anonymous. The strangers here are strangers. As they should be.

Standing by the chessboards in Washington Square Park
I was approached by a blue-eyed kid selling used discs and
bootleg tapes. "Very rare," he said. He wore sandals and
anklets and eyeliner. The skin on his knees was ash white and
dirty; he had freckles on his forehead, frizzy blond hair pushed
through a rubber band. I told him to get lost, but he persisted.
He said if I wanted something else, anything at all, he could
probably get it. He said he knew people. I asked if people knew
him, and he said not really. Then he asked if I knew people.
I said I didn't.

Benna is in fact not Benna, but Beatrice. She changed her
name after learning the whole truth about the woman she's
named after. It makes you think about everyone you ever
knew, and how different they might be with different names.
I once knew a girl who went from Nicole to Nika, thinking it
more exceptional. But Nika wasn't, and never would be,
exceptional. She wasn't even good.

The girl born Nicole Rabian wore icy lipstick, lace gloves,
high heels, and half shirts; her hair was often pink and sometimes gold or platinum. The youngest kid of a single mom, she
was given an extra-long leash and permission to roam with
impunity. She had two older brothers, twins named Teddy
and Eddie. Nika and Eddie were the scourges of the neighborhood, notorious for tagging walls and fences with Magnum-44
markers, throwing golf balls through library windows, and
most famously for blowing up a four-month-old German
shepherd with an M-80. Teddy was the quiet one.

First in her class to kiss, cheat, smoke, and steal, Nika became the pace car for experimentation — the most looked-at
girl in school. One of her protéges was Jorden, then the new

girl in eighth grade. Nika sensed potential and opened her crooked wing to the outsider. The two were tight for weeks, but things turned nasty after Nika rolled over and told everyone about the homemade breast jam.

"Is it working?" asked Nika, the girls dressed in robes in her basement, the ointment rubbed into their chests.

"Can't you feel the tingle?" said Jorden. "That's blood rushing."

"That's good?"

"Yeah, like when boys get boners."

"That *is* good!"

Made from camphor, white wax, spermaceti, and Mediterranean mint oil, the age-old blend, if applied at the right time of month with the appropriate invocation, was said to stimulate growth of the mammary glands. Some other girls in class were all ears, eager to learn how they too could pump up their profiles. They even bought a few jars of the stuff, wrapped in a label of Nika's design. But the jars wound up on the front steps of school, adorned with Jorden's photo, the word *witch* written huge on her forehead.

Conferences were called, silent treatments ensued, and the new girl suffered at the petty hands of minions turned mean by propaganda. They stole her gym clothes, called her a lesbian, hid her bookbag in the sewer.

Page 1463: color-coded gray

9/27/87

Everyone hates the new girl now. She and Nika were best friends but not anymore. Nika's cruel but pretty. People've been saying she shaves her pubes to look like an equilateral triangle. She blamed Jorden for the rumor and launched a war. Now the kids say she bakes witch cakes and steals kittens. I don't say that stuff, though.

Two days later, in a brash effort to broaden her constituency, Nika recruited Henry, and despite the opinions he expressed in his ledger on September 27, he went willingly into the folds of eighth-grade royalty. Henry was never a popular boy—unknown as opposed to unliked. But there he was, one of the with-it kids, making voodoo dolls and drinking Kahlua in Nika's furnished basement, stealing sunglasses, Walkmans, and rhinestone Swatches from the Chestnut Hill Mall.

It lasted about a week. He dropped out after witnessing an incident at the local park.

Page 1472: color-coded red

10/3/87

Eddie Rabian is five minutes older than Teddy and never lets him forget it. Eddie keeps the back of his head shaved. He lets the top grow out, dyes it orange, and slicks it back through a rubber band. The tail hangs down a few inches. He has a tattoo of a snake farm on the back of his neck. He says it's a snake farm, but it looks more like a sun or something. He's fifteen, the dominator of the family, bigger and smarter than Teddy, and very protective of Nika. Truth is, Teddy is probably a pretty nice guy, but even if he was, Eddie and Nika would never let him be.

Today I saw them on the steps of the dried-out fountain in the park. I was far away so they couldn't see me. Occasionally Eddie called out, "Everybody be quiet, I'm hunting turtle!" or "The turtle sucks dick!" or "Kill the turtle!" Nika laughed, egging him on. He was yelling at a quiet man sitting on the opposite side of the fountain. The guy was in a wheelchair, maybe twenty years old, wearing a white dress shirt, gray pants, blue tie, gold watch, black sneakers, and a turtle mask, the plastic kind you buy at a drug store.

"She wants to stroke your tail!" screamed Eddie, grabbing and shaking Nika, who laughed. Teddy just kind of sat there, looking uncomfortable, like he didn't know where to look.

"Push out your tail, freak!" yelled Nika. The turtle-man stayed still and silent, his knees together, holding a large brown paper bag. Nika stood and pulled up Eddie's shorts leg, showing off his tattoo of a terrapin. "You're no turtle," she told him. "*Here's* your fuckin' turtle!"

This type of call-and-no-response went on for about ten minutes. Eddie and Nika yelled and laughed, Teddy kept quiet, and the turtle-man just bobbed his head, like *fuck you all.* Then, as the tension was rising, the attention turned to a crowd forming around Alton Hauser, a local newscaster with orangey skin and sunglasses, who had just rolled into the park on a pair of skates. Eddie went over to shake hands with the celebrity, then pulled up his shirt and asked for an autographed stomach. As this was happening, the turtle-man slipped away and wheeled over to the edge of the park. I followed him.

He removed his mask, shirt, tie, and watch, and dropped them into the brown paper bag. Then he stood up, as if nothing were wrong with his legs. He left his wheelchair and, dressed in an untucked white T-shirt and black-rimmed glasses, walked back to the fountain and stood right near the Rabians. Eddie — shirtless now and very proud of his temporary tattoo — didn't notice. None of them did.

The next day Henry stopped Jorden on her way out of school. "You going to the dance place at the mall?"

Jorden, of late a target for hurtful pranks, said nothing and kept on walking. Her book bag had been replaced by a backpack firmly fastened around her shoulders, a pair of tap shoes dangling from the strap. Henry later discovered the pack contained a rape whistle and a canister of Mace.

"Isn't there a cake store near there?" asked Henry. He knew there was a bakery next to the studio.

They'd seen each other around but never really spoke. She knew, of course, that lately he'd been running with Nika.

"Those tapping shoes?" asked Henry.

Jorden didn't answer.

"I made tapping shoes once. With seashells."

She didn't break stride.

"You any good?" he asked. "I wasn't, but I could see you being good." He looked admiringly at the shoes. "You know if they got any good cake over there?"

She turned to face him. "Pretty good." And she turned back to the sidewalk.

"Yeah?"

"Not bad," she said.

"What's your favorite?" asked Henry. "What's your favorite kind of cake?"

Jorden shrugged.

"Chocolate cake? Cheesecake?"

Jorden showed more emotion for the former, but remained on guard.

"Lemon?"

That was the one, he could tell.

"Lemon?" said Henry. "You like lemon cake?"

She nodded.

"I like cinnamon buns," he said. "My mom used to make them. With extra icing. The more icing the better, right?"

"I have a roll of quarters," said Jorden, pulling a weighty paper cylinder from her pocket. She squeezed it snug in her palm. "If you hold it like this, when you punch someone there's less chance you'll break a bone."

For a second, Henry thought she was threatening him.

"I transcribe interviews for my dad," she said. "He's kind of a rock doctor, for gems and stuff. He pays me in quarters."

"My dad's a doctor, too!" said Henry. "Well, he used to be. For people, though. For their skin."

Jorden handed him the quarters. Henry told her about the time he punched lamps wearing his father's lead-lined gloves. He gripped the roll and punched himself a few times in the leg.

"Yeah," he said, punching harder, then again, harder. "Solid."

"Careful," said Jorden. "You'll bruise."

6

Henry's eighth grade teacher was a bitter mistress, twice divorced, always on the latest diet. It was widely gossiped that she pined for the principal, and that he occasionally pined her in his office, after school. Her name was Miss Booey and she hated Henry's whistling. He was quite talented, blowing bebop skats as easily as the latest pop tune, laying down the occasional original on a bedroom tape recorder. Not that he'd ever play them for anyone.

"Must you *whis*tle all the time?" said Miss Booey as Henry strolled the hall, hands in his pockets, Vince Guaraldi's "Red Baron" coruscating off his lips. He had taken to strolling in his thirteenth year, assuming the air of a retiree, referring to himself as an "old soul." He dressed comfortably, often in cruisewear—sun hats, sandals, drawstring pants—and began crossing his legs as he sat in class. He watched game shows, ate herring, drank borscht, called girls "dames," pinched his peers' cheeks, sat down while he peed, even once tried wearing Depends, but the convenience wasn't worth it.

"What of it?" he said, looking up at Miss Booey.

She bent down, stuck out her neck, and tilted her head.

Henry could see rouge grounds in the grooves of her face. "You don't see me announcing to the world how happy I am, do you? Have some boundaries."

"I could whistle sad songs," offered Henry.

As it happened, on that particular late-autumn day, Henry had wanted to whistle sad songs. The bad news was piling up. His father was taking over his former playroom, using the space to build a massive saltwater aquarium for lethal breeds of jellyfish. "We need the room," said Dad, and by "we" he meant himself and the Cnidarians. "Some o' these blobs'll grow over six feet wide!"

He said he was going to tame them.

Henry wasn't against the tank or the taming—he liked jellyfish—but his playroom was off limits. He'd always had permission to draw on the walls, and there was barely a space he hadn't filled with some significant scribble. Consumed these days with a premature nostalgia, the thirteen-year-old couldn't bear the thought of losing the walls—or "scrolls," as he'd taken to calling them. He mounted protests, slept in the playroom, taped "Save the Scrolls" posters around the house. But Dad was firm: "No can do." The walls would be stripped and painted deep blue and sea green to make the animals feel more at home.

"What about *me* feeling at home?" said Henry.

"You've lived here your whole life," said Dad.

On top of that, Henry's gym teacher, a lanky, bearded man named Mr. Van Putt, would be calling the house. That afternoon, Henry made it into the Monkey Club by climbing the rope using only his upper body. An achievement, to be sure, but he stayed up there, refusing to come down, insisting on breaking the school record.

"We don't *have* a school record," said Mr. Van Putt, dressed in his signature red Fila warm-up, looking up at Henry, who was a few inches from the forty-foot ceiling.

"I'm setting one!" he called out.

"You've al*ready* set it! Come offa there!"

"I'm setting it *big*ger!"

His classmates crowded around the mats below the rope, craning their necks to watch the record breaker.

Mr. Van Putt looked at his watch. There were fifteen minutes left in the period. In the name of sport, he was prepared to let it slide. But when the bell rang and Henry stayed put, the game was called. As was common in moments like this, Henry heard those *Great Ovations* in his head.

"I am *not* kidding," said Mr. Van Putt, his next class filing into the gym. "Down, Henry! Now!"

"I'm achieving—"

"*Now!*" yelled the teacher, gripping the rope.

"Please don't shake the rope," said Henry, citing safety rule number one.

Forty minutes later the principal assured Henry that his father would be called to discuss an insolence that had gone from dogged to dangerous. But what really worried Henry was the exposure of his secret strength. Scared of becoming a vicarious vessel, he'd always played it weedy in front of Dad. If found out, the old man would surely beam at the prospects for his new and improved son—he'd want him to fill cracks in the driveway, assemble and install things, work on his swing.

And finally, as if all this weren't enough, there were the mysterious letters. Henry was on permanent mail duty at home, a welcome chore as he was always on the lookout for Mom's weekly missive. The day before, though, he received the second of two puzzling warnings from the government, slips of paper with the words CONTRABAND SEIZED written in capital letters. What was seized, they didn't say. Henry panicked, his mind jumping from crime to crime. Drugs? Pornography? Plutonium? There were, of course, no return addresses.

Jorden had some theories on how to duck the rope-climbing incident. "Plead fear," she said, leaning against the bike rack after school. "Just tell him you were too scared to come down."

"Scared of what?" said Henry.

"Falling, burning your hands."

"But how do I explain the strength? I don't want to wind up in the park on weekends or doing fix ups around the house. I know you think he's an original, but when it comes to dad stuff he goes out of his way to be regular."

She spoke slowly, instructively. "When a person gets scared, they can perform unusual feats of strength. It's called the 'fight or flight' response. They produce more adrenaline, their heart speeds up—"

"Fight or flight?"

"Just tell him your arms locked and the yelling made it worse."

"Are those real terms? He's a doctor, he knows all about glands and stuff."

Jorden gave him a look: *It's me you're talking to here.*

"Okay," said Henry, taking off his golf cap and smoothing back his hair that was glazed with Vitalis. "Fight or flight —I'll use it." He put the cap back on. "Now what about the letters?"

7

Who are you?

This was the topic for the eighth grade essay contest and the impetus for Henry's plan to topple the monstrous Nika. All entries had to be typed and were due before Christmas vacation. The winner's piece would be published in the local paper on New Year's Day, and the author would receive a two-hundred-dollar gift certificate to Blue Mountain Creamery, a sweets store famous for its fudge. If all went well, Nika would soon be a published essayist in need of a pile of napkins—and they wouldn't be for her mouth.

But before taking aim, Henry felt he needed to work out his own answers to the essay question. The metaphysical topic struck a chord and he found himself starting at the Precambrian era and sifting through four and a half billion years worth of *being*, contemplating cranial capacity, pondering the earlobe, tracing back his belly button, double checking his thumbs and toes. Henry was always cloudy about matters of the self. He didn't trust mirrors. On registration forms, under ethnic background, he'd always check "Other." At night he'd lie awake and ask *Hello?* He'd always felt faulty, incomplete— as if his insides didn't match his outsides.

11/2/87

Today in gym we played basketball — shirts and skins. I hate being skins. Some kids really like it — they can't wait to take off their shirts. One of these kids, very muscly, said, "You are so white!" when I jumped for a rebound. Some other kids laughed, as if this was the funniest thing in the world. A real insult. I thought it was an insult, too, but for different reasons. Well, maybe not an insult. It's not that I feel black or brown or red or yellow — it's not a matter of color at all. I just don't feel like the front-runner. I don't feel part of the majority.

Finally, after standing on one leg while reading a biographical dictionary in an attempt to force a moment of clarity, it all came clear. Henry wasn't that old a soul. Deep down, he was an outcast, a buccaneer. And not just any. According to the dictionary, "Every, Henry" was the arch pirate of a golden age that terrorized early eighteenth-century seas.

"I'm also known as Long Ben," he told Jorden. They were in her room, making paper airplanes. Henry's was painted black, a white skull and crossbones on each wing.

"I won't argue," she said. "I'd hate to walk the plank."

"Argh," growled Henry, waving away her concern. "We pirates rarely, if ever, make prisoners walk the plank. I'd be more worried about keelhauling and marooning, if I were you."

"Marooning?"

"Once I forced a captive to eat his own ears."

"You did that?"

He wondered. "I think it was me."

"What's marooning?"

"Leaving someone somewhere to die. Like on a desert island or something."

"Is that the plan for Nika?"

"Yup. But we're gonna leave her right where she is."

"Why not a desert island? With wolves and lizards?"

"Because," said Henry, "we want the kids to eat her."

Jorden gave her pink plane a toss and watched it crash into the wall. On contact, she heard an awful, muffled wail coming from the upstairs bathroom.

"You hear that?" she asked Henry.

He was busy cutting spikes into the tail of his plane.

Jorden got up and walked down the hall to the bathroom. The door was closed. "Dad?" she called. "You okay?"

"I'm fine, honey," he said from behind the door. "Just stretching."

It didn't sound like stretching, but she didn't want to pry. They were very respectful of each other's space. She listened for another few seconds, heard nothing, and walked back down the hall to her room.

"Hey!" she yelled, standing in the doorway. Her airplane was colored black, a skull and crossbones painted on each wing. Henry was holding a scissors, a paper patch taped over his eye.

The plan was simple. Henry and Jorden would compose a first-rate, soul-bearing essay "by Nicole Rabian" and submit it for entry in the contest. Nika would get a surprise on New Year's Day, the star exposed for all her vicious edges, the real witch sent to the gallows. The tricky part was assuring its publication in the paper. Henry suggested bribing the class's heavy hitters, asking them to take a fall for the greater good.

"Too risky," said Jorden, pad and pencil in hand. "You have to hide your cards — kids would talk. Besides, I can write a winner."

"Positively?"

"With your help? Absolutely."

"Who'll do what?"

"You're big picture guy — the man with the plan."

"You report to me?"

"Correct."

"Okay then," said Henry, rolling up his sleeves. "We've got two weeks till deadline. I want an outline — *with* ideas for illustrations — in my locker by nine o'clock Monday morning."

"Monday?"

"Problem?" said Henry, looking down his nose at her.

Jorden smiled, happy to be challenged.

8

Dad was wearing his new stinger suit. It was an insulated Lycra diving skin with reinforced stitching to protect against the jellyfish's nematocysts. In the suit, one could move freely among the animals without fear of envenomation. (This was of particular concern to Henry's father; as a kid he went into anaphylactic shock from a bee sting.) There were, however, no tanks yet in the Every residence, just a bunch of fish books and a case of vinegar. Dad simply enjoyed wearing the suit.

Henry was by now well aware that "jellies" were here before the dinosaurs, that they're 96 percent water, heartless, spineless, and brainless, and that they kill more people annually than snakes or sharks. He knew that male jellies release sperm through their mouths, the bioluminescent Comb jelly glows blue in the dark, and that the Upside-down jelly grows its own food (algae) in its belly. He'd been told that the tentacles of the Lion's Mane can drag up to two hundred feet, and that despite its tiny size, the Irukandji is perhaps the most dangerous, much more so than the dreaded Portuguese man of war (which, technically, isn't even a jellyfish). Such marine minutiae had taken over their conversations, but Henry now had missions to accomplish. He was out there on land, trying to make things better, he and Jorden, for the greater good.

"Pinch me," said Dad, holding out his arm, showing off the toughness of the material.

"No," said Henry.

"Come on," said Dad. "Pinch."

"You look like a crazy person."

"I'm in-de-*struct*ible," said Dad in a superhero voice. And then in his regular voice: "My helmet's coming soon in the mail."

"How can you tame a brainless fish?"

"They're not *fish*. They're Cnidarians."

"How can you tame a brainless *anything*?"

Dad said nothing.

Henry stayed fixed on the helmet. *Is that what the contraband letters were about? A stupid helmet?*

"Are we expecting anything else in the mail?"

"Got a call from Mr. Van Putt last night."

The old sneak attack, deadpan and deadly.

Henry wrinkled. "Van what?"

"Putt," said Dad. "Your gym teacher."

"Ah," said Henry. "Right. Kind of a *nah-nee nah-nee boo-boo*, Van Putt, but . . ."

"Stop dancing, Slippy." Dad called him "Slippy" when he tried to wiggle out of a situation.

"But I was going for the *record*."

"He told you to get down."

"Yes, but I was *achieving*. On a *grand scale*."

"What about the bell? Class ended."

"There's six a day!"

"Did you break the record?"

A tricky question. "Define break."

"Anyone stay up there longer than you?"

"Nope."

"Ever?"

Henry felt quite sure. "Never."

"Impressive," said Dad, doing deep knee bends, testing the elasticity of the suit. "Thought I had a goose egg for a boy."

Uh-oh, thought Henry. He backpedaled. "My arms just kind of locked. I was scared of falling, burning my hands."

"That'll happen," said Dad.

"I could have really ruptured myself."

Dad smirked, rolling his knee.

"I don't think I could do it again."

Dad swung his arms around in giant circles. "Listen, can you help me bring some stuff up from the basement?"

Henry took a last shot: "Have you ever heard of the fight or flight response?"

The mailman came late that Friday. He usually reached the Every house at 1:15, while Henry was at school. But today there was a detour and the two practically bumped into each other.

"Hiya, kid," said the mailman. Skinny with a doughboy gut, he was an ex-milkman named Barry who wore tinted glasses and chewed toothpicks, the type of guy who took pride in his wornout concert T-shirts and still kept his high school bong in the closet.

"Hi," said Henry.

"Got a package for you." Barry handed over a box about the size of a head; the return address said See the Sea, Inc.

"Can I ask you something?"

Barry smiled, the toothpick between his teeth. "You want to be a mailman when you grow up?"

"No, it's—"

"Lotsa kids wanna be mailmen when they grow up. I tell 'em they better think *three* times before making that decision."

Henry had a million questions about what constitutes contraband, but he got the sense that Barry was enjoying this mentor thing. So instead of getting briefed on U.S. Postal procedures, he indulged the man and asked about vicious dogs.

"Oh, sure, dogs are part of the game, but they're knee-high to a grasshopper out here. I was attacked by a *goat*." Barry seemed very proud of this, like he'd taken a bullet for a cause. "Hadda get a rabies shot and everything. Didn't deliver any more mail on *that* day."

Henry jumped on the segue. "What would be considered really wrong to deliver in the mail? Besides the obvious, like guns and stuff. What else could you get in trouble for?"

Barry squinted. "You a sympathizer?"

Henry was only vaguely aware of what that meant, but he knew it was bad. "I've lived here my whole life," he said. "My dad's a doctor."

"I'm a mailman, what's the difference?"

"I've gotten a couple of these letters, *contra*band letters—"

"I seen 'em," said Barry, as if he knew all along. "Could be any number of things."

"What kind of things?"

"Pharmaceuticals, trademark violations, body parts—"

"Body parts?"

"You'd have to call Customs, down in D.C. Wouldn't be surprised if they showed up asking *you* some questions."

With that frightening and unhelpful hint, Barry handed Henry the stack of mail and walked back into battle as if they were no closer as human beings than they were an hour ago. On top was the weekly letter from Mom. As usual it was handwritten on peach-colored stationery, ant stickers placed with random precision around the words.

December 7, 1987

Greetings, golden boy! I have just returned from a trip to Notodden, which is located in the South East part of Norway. I went with a new girlfriend of mine, Leslie. She's a botanist from Amsterdam who's here growing baobab trees. They're very funny trees, the fattest you've ever seen and shaped like a bottle. They're pollinated by bats, they blossom only in moonlight, and their fruit is called monkey bread. They're really terrific trees. You'd like them a lot. Remember when we lined up the milk bottles and went bowling with grapefruits? That's what they remind me of.

I miss you awful. Yesterday I walked by the front of a school near my apartment. A group of children stood in front of a yellow bus and argued about who was going to be whose partner on a field trip they were making. A blond girl said to an Asian girl, "But you just *have* to be my partner," to which the Asian girl replied, "I do not." It made me think of you.

Well, off I go for supper—salmon fish and rice. I've become much less neurotic about food. You'd be proud.

LOVE, LOVE, LOVE,

Mamma

9

By nine o'clock Monday morning there was a typed draft of the essay in Henry's locker, spiral-bound with a laminated cover page and indexed illustrations of a ketchup bottle, a tube of toothpaste, a Vidalia onion, and a lemon. Jorden had placed a yellow Post-it on the front explaining that she'd composed the essay in the form of a diary entry "because it will seem more original/personal/naked/authentic."

Dear Diary,

I remember watching *Gulliver's Travels* as a little girl and wanting to become a giant so my footsteps shook the earth. One night, many Januarys ago, my uncle convinced me he was a genie and that I could have but one special wish. I chose to be the biggest, fiercest giant in the land.

He blindfolded me, put on my mittens, scarf, hat, and coat, and picked me up in his padded arms. After a long walk he put me down. I had no idea where I was. He took the blindfold off and left me standing in the middle of a frozen lake.

"Behold, Gulliver!" he shouted.

And there I was, on top of the big wide world, slipping and sliding from continent to continent. I spun around, my arms outstretched, my huge feet making canyons in the snow. My breath was like the wind. I played connect the dots with the stars.

"But I don't see any *other* giants," I said.

"That's how much bigger you are."

He was right. I used to be bigger than all of you. But I'm shrinking.

This morning I heard "Karma Chameleon" on the radio while I was getting dressed. It made me think about this essay contest. I looked up the words in the dictionary. *Karma* refers to the path you choose in life, the goodness/badness of your actions and how they'll determine your fate. According to your karma, you could be reincarnated as a powerful president (if you're good), a dirty rat (if you're bad), or anything in between. Chameleons, of course, are lizards, but in the song I think it means a person who is always changing. That's me.

When I was younger, not so long ago, I had a lot of nervous energy. I'd suck on my hair and get fur balls in my stomach. I'd punch my stuffed animals in the face. I had problems wetting my bed. This is a very bad problem for most kids, but not for me. See, it wasn't an accident, as they kept saying. I *chose* to do it. I liked the cold, wet sheets. I liked the smell. I still do it sometimes. *So what?* So what if I still like to pick my nose and eat it? So what if I have a crush on Mr. Van Putt? So what if I pretend to be someone I'm not?

Olly-olly-oxen-free! Come out, come out, wherever you are!

Maybe I did bad in my past life. Why else would I get

lice? I've spread rumors, I've made people cry. I've experimented on animals, killed thousands of bugs. I stole a girl's puppy, waited for the reward signs, then returned it and collected the money. Once I tried to set my napping brother on fire by holding a magnifying glass between his back and the sun. *Who am I?* Good question.

We're all people, but what kind? We all have things in common—breathing, eating, we all have hearts and noses—so what's the difference? How different can one thing be? Is ketchup just for burgers? Is toothpaste just for teeth? Is lemon just for fish and lemonade? No, no, and no. I clean my pennies with ketchup. I put toothpaste on my pimples. I suck on lemons for motion sickness. See what I mean? Cucumbers are fruits, not vegetables. So are pumpkins, eggplants, squash, and tomatoes. *Lucifer* means "light bearer." Things are not as they seem.

Who am I? Who knows? I changed my name to Nika, I wear lifts in my shoes, I get bikini waxes. I'm a giant. I'm an onion. I'm Abraham Lincoln. I'm John Wilkes Booth. Did you know that Booth was the greatest matinee idol of his era?

I'm a rumor that I started.

"Fantastic!" said Henry, holding the essay up to the sun as if to check its veracity.

"Thanks," said Jorden, leaning against the bike rack.

"Love the drawings," he said, examining the onion sketch: a cross section, showing its layers.

"Thought you would."

"Was John Wilkes Booth really a movie star?"

"Well, they didn't have movies back then, but he was a stage star, yeah. Got bags of fan letters."

"How d'you know that?"

"Just do," said Jorden—her usual response to that question.

"Where'd you get that Gulliver stuff?"

Jorden paused. "Her diary."

"From when you were friends?"

"No," she said, taking a breath. "Yesterday."

Henry looked puzzled. "How?"

"Couldn't get started," she said. "I needed a lead."

"Not following."

"Don't worry," said Jorden.

It was here that Henry found out his partner in crime was actually a criminal.

"You broke into her house?"

Jorden shrugged, forced a smile. "I didn't *break* in."

"She'll know it's missing."

"I didn't *steal* it," said Jorden. "Just copied down some notes."

"She'll *know*," said Henry. "She'll know it was *some*one."

"There are things to be scared of—this isn't one of them."

"Have you met her brothers?"

"She'll never know."

"What's there to be scared of?"

"*Nothing.*"

"You just said there were things to be scared of. Like what?"

"Oh," said Jorden, thinking big. "Mushroom clouds, AIDS . . . getting kidnapped . . . Ethiopia . . ."

"How'd you get in and out of her room without being seen?"

"Easy," she said.

Jorden was tiptoeing and Henry could tell. There was something else, something bigger. The moment turned slo-mo. Henry's face went slack. He was right in the middle of an epiphany and Jorden knew exactly what it was.

"He de*served* it," she said, a preemptive strike. She breathed deep, accountable, not sure if she was about to be pelted.

Henry squinted, his jaw hung heavy. It clicked: "You wrecked my cow!"

"It was wrecking *you!* It was driving you crazy!"

Henry rewound to the night with the cinnamon and sugar. "How did you get there so fast? Where was my dad?"

"He actually found me in your room."

"You two were in ca*hoots?!*"

"No!"

"And my fucking cow! You *three* were in cahoots!"

"I told him I was playing a prank and he let it go!"

"I thought it was *him* this whole time. I didn't say anything because I didn't want to give him the satis*fac*tion!" Henry took a deep breath. He felt pain and then rage and then sadness. He stormed off.

That night, he didn't return any of her many phone calls. But by morning all his hurt feelings had morphed into mischief. He walked over to Jorden's house and threw a twig at her window. She leaned out. "Can you teach me?" said Henry.

The world shrank ten sizes that day. All the pockets, drawers, and closets were instantaneously denuded, their private, cluttered insides up for grabbing, free of charge. Fences wilted, windows melted, locks were shrunk and cracked. Just one rule: *No stealing.*

"It's a black bag job," said Jorden. "We're free to browse,

free to sit in chairs and roll on beds and flip through albums, books, and fridges: but no stealing, *ever*. Not even a piece of candy."

"It goes against my pirate nature," warned Henry, as if he couldn't possibly help who he was. "Sometimes I plunder."

"Well, TATB," she said, an acronym for "those are the breaks." "That's the one big rule. Agreed?"

Henry nodded, just like his dad. "So what's the mission?"

"No mission."

"What's the point of browsing? Why risk it?"

"I like it," said Jorden.

"Like what about it?"

"I don't know," she said. "Makes you feel . . . normal. *More* normal."

"How?"

"What do you hate about yourself?"

Henry paused to think. "Lots of stuff."

"Like?"

"My hipbone's too sharp, my right eye's lazy—"

"Not outside things, *in*side things."

"Oh," said Henry. The question had an answer, one he thought of often, but it was in the back of his brain somewhere, inchoate, too big to break down. It bubbled when he eavesdropped on the black kids who were bused in from the black areas, or when he watched the deaf girl cleaning her hearing aid, or when the wheelchair kids talked about wheelchairs. He felt it when he read about Native American rituals, Hasidim, gang initiations, and when he first learned about the Amish with their black hats and buggies. Henry found his own world too roomy, too vague. He wanted real kinship, community, to be part of an "us," but an "us" who are unlike others. He boiled it down to a word: "Status?"

"The most commonly used word in the English language is *I*."

"What does that prove?"

"That people are self-obsessed, always looking to move on, move out."

"They're looking to move *up* — that's the difference."

"You're looking to move *down?*"

"In status, yes."

"Down where? Toward what?"

"The minority," said Henry, tracing the grain of his fingerprints, very aware of being a healthy, young, straight white male sitting on green grass outside a red-brick school. "Something smaller, something *other*."

10

"Gin and bear it," his wife used to say, by way of an admonition. He'd always enjoyed a Scotch, but gin was Harlan's steady, especially in the weeks following the funeral. Gin and the ledger. He drank and drank and wondered from which chain of DNA his boy had pulled this will to write. *He had something to prove*, thought Harlan and at times even second-guessed the corpse, thinking it part of a larger plan to teach a lesson. *But what?*

As the glasses piled up, it was harder for him to read in sequence. He'd want to jump ahead, skip the maudlin parts about the disappointment of finally getting to say the F-word, or the recondite rant on why sunbathing was dishonest. It was a tricky read, tangential and vague, and often way too frank. But he admired the scope, the diligence with which it was crafted. He pledged out loud to the ledger itself: "You have my undivided attention." He promised to hear out every word, in sequence. He even tried recording some of his own observations, red ink on graph paper, just like Henry, an attempt to better grasp the author's mind and methods. It didn't yield much.

I am not a writer. He didn't get it from me.

Harlan poked through old pants pockets, pulled out drawers, and rummaged through closets, searching the house for extra clues into Henry's character. He missed him. More upsetting, he'd missed out on him. For someone who kept everything where it belonged, it was particularly tragic that he'd lost his son. He'd hold pictures of Henry's face next to his own and stare in the mirror, noting the resemblance. He'd write their names next to each other again and again on paper. He was taking an interest, making an effort. But sometimes the gulf just seemed too big, as if he were reading the notes of a stranger. And at times it rang too true.

Page 1543: color-coded pink

12/10/87
Dad's strength is uncrushable. He can deal with anything.
Except failure. God help him if he ever has to deal with that.

Harlan sat back, drunk, and sank his head into the sofa. He stared at his fisheyed reflection in the turned-off TV. He thought about hurling the mug, smashing his face, but it felt like a cliché—worse, it was the type of cliché that Henry would have hated. He felt good for recognizing this and fell gently into sleep, the ledger opened to page 1602, logged in mid-December, color-coded purple for "pride."

"The plan is up and running," wrote Henry. "Jorden mailed the essay this morning. All we can do now is wait. Jorden said comeuppance was coming. I was embarrassed to admit I didn't know what that meant."

11

If Henry and Jorden harbored any guilt about their plan to dethrone Nika, their consciences were cleaned in the days before Christmas vacation. The little basilisk went savage, adding insults and injuries to her list of foul deeds. "Santa isn't coming," she said, "so fuck him and the sleigh he rode in on."

"Santa hears you," said Liberty, a lipstickless classmate with blond braids and Quaker parents.

"Do you like candy canes?" asked Nika.

"Yes," said Liberty.

"Did you know if you suck the end too sharp it can pop your tongue?"

Liberty gasped, horrified.

"Want one?" asked Nika.

Liberty nodded. "I'll be careful."

Earlier, during recess, Nika had dragged the candy through the dirt and left it sitting on the grass as bait for beetle-bugs and ants. She told Liberty to "open up and close your eyes." Liberty opened wide. For a second the texture was pleasant, alive, like Pop Rocks or Fizz. Then she gagged, the insects filling her mouth, crawling all over her teeth and tongue. Nika howled as Liberty choked and spit out all her saliva, wiping her mouth on her forearms as she sprinted for the water fountain.

The following day, during a safety lecture on Bunsen burners, the science teacher told Nika to be quiet — she was whispering to a popular boy with bangs and a hoop earring. She responded by saying, "I just thought my classmates should know that Jorden and Henry are dating and doing things."

Everyone giggled and looked at the lab partners huddled close in the corner by the beakers. They were used to the imputation, Nika having made it top news over the past two weeks, but Jorden wasn't in the mood. She stood up, angry. Henry pulled her down.

"What?" she said, fired up.

"Hide your cards," whispered Henry.

Hearing her own advice made sense. She remained seated.

After school, the scene was set for a beheading. The basement door was locked, the Ping-Pong table covered with a sacrificial sheet. Candles burned, incense smoked, Bartók played low on a boom box. Jorden and Henry wore bathrobes over hooded sweatshirts, their faces turned tribal by makeup and mud.

"Where'd you get the guillotine?"

"My dad used to collect weapons," said Henry. "He scrapped the hobby, but this was a keeper. It's a mini, but the blade's pretty heavy."

"Handsome," she said, touching the piece.

"After the weapons, he was obsessed with animal rituals." Henry told Jorden the tales he'd been told: that in the Middle Ages it was not uncommon for "guilty" beasts to be tried and publicly executed. Birds, wolves, pigs, insects—they were all fair game, capable of heresy as defined by the ecclesiastical courts. The poor things suffered excommunication, torture, and death, which was the sentence to be carried out today. "I'm pretty sure it ended in seventeen-something when a French judge hung a cow for sorcery."

"It's 'hanged,'" said Jorden.

"The French were the worst; that's what my dad says." Henry continued speaking as he prepared the guillotine. "This judge once shredded a pig's legs for murdering a little girl, then hanged it, then dragged it through town, dressed up in the girl's jacket."

"Gross," said Jorden, staring at Moo, thinking of Nika. The convict was sequestered in a cardboard jail.

"The big difference between condemned animals and people was that people tipped their executioners."

"What for?"

"Clean cuts," said Henry. "Mary Queen of Scots, it took fifteen whacks."

Jorden cringed and rubbed the top bone of her spine. "Who's Mary Queen of Scots?"

"Not sure," said Henry, tightening his hood, a little surprised that Jorden didn't know. "But my dad said it took fifteen whacks." He raised the blade. "I think we're all set here."

Jorden ceremoniously freed Moo and kissed her (Henry said it was a "her") on the nose. Henry stared longingly into her eyes, seeing his smaller self in the plastic pupils. The cow would die, and with her a heap of secrets. There was no better witness to Henry's life so far, and that's what ultimately sealed her fate. Moo knew too much. And she was guilty of being in cahoots. It was a dangerous combination.

Jorden laid a hand towel over the bench and gently placed the bovine flat on her stomach, her throat lined up with the edge. "Last words?"

The cow kept silent. Henry squeezed her rump. There it was, the old familiar *moo*. Salty-eyed, he thought of pardoning his old pal but quickly canned the mercy. He put her back on the block, steadied himself, and looked at Jorden, who gave the nod to proceed.

The blade fell fast. Moo's head popped off and rolled, sending Henry into the next phase of his life. Jorden picked it up and handed it to the executioner. The skull was impaled on a spiked broomstick and stuck in a terracotta pot filled with sand. Henry kept the token in his room, a harbinger to heretics, a sign that he'd accepted fate and purpose as design.

12

The jellyfish tanks came early, New Year's morning, a little later than scheduled because of the commotion a few blocks away. There were cops, a crime scene investigator, a medical examiner, and the television crew for Alton Hauser.

"What happened?" asked the tank man, dressed in a baggy turquoise jumpsuit, his baseball hat decorated with little bubbles.

Henry's father didn't seem particularly concerned. "Is this it? Is this everything?"

The tank man checked his clipboard. "Better be." He tried looking past the customer, into the house. "You starting an aquarium in there?"

"Where's the Kreisel?" Henry's father pointed to a massive box. "Is that it?" He was referring to the cylindrical tank necessary to simulate a sealike laminar flow. The tank man shrugged. He kept turning back toward the sirens.

"Henry!" yelled Dad. "Henry, get down here! I need help!"

Henry was upstairs, nervous, looking out the window. This was a momentous day for him, too. The paper went to press, the winner of the essay contest spelled out big beneath the fold. It was a day of reckoning, like in the spring of 1694, when Long Ben Every, a slaver employed by the Royal Governor of Bermuda, took charge of a ship and sailed it into legend.

The captain was sloshed on punch, passed out in his bed, when Long Ben and his mutineers secured the hatches, pulled the anchor, and set out into the Atlantic. The captain awoke to the rock of the waves. "What's the matter?" he said. "What weather is it?"

"No, no," answered Long Ben. "We're at sea. Come, don't be in a fright. Put on your clothes and I'll let you into a secret. You must know that I am the captain of this ship now. And this is my cabin."

From that night forth, the crew obeyed a different voice. The captain was left for dead, the sloop rechristened the *Fancy*, and a new flag was raised to the winds—red, with four silver chevrons. The name of Every would soon top the Royal Navy's most wanted list, striking fright in the hearts of seafarers from the Bay of Bengal to the Cape of Good Hope.

And yet, despite the pluck and valor of his former self, this newer Henry Every was scared. Scared to look at the paper. Scared of all the sirens.

"Henry!" yelled his father.

Henry went into the bathroom and closed the door. He took off his shirt and stared at his armpits in the mirror, taking stock of new hairs, new smells. His face looked drained and ashy. His skull felt wobbly. The sirens kept coming, crosshatched like a round he used to sing in chorus. He remembered something that Jorden had said: Spiders have transparent blood. "Am I a spider?" he thought.

Meanwhile over at Jorden's, the breakfast links were cut,

the eggs browned just right in butter, the oranges freshly squeezed into a crystal pitcher. Her dad was lately eating bigger meals, at all hours, and dessert after each one. His circumference was growing, you could see it in his fingers, but Jorden saw increased appetite as a positive sign — "A zest," she said, "and zest is good."

"Pass the preserves," said her dad, pointing to his favorite, the Very Cherry marmalade boiled at the bakery near the dance place. He spread the fruit over a waffle, then added maple syrup, fresh whipped cream, and powdered sugar. His mouth full, he asked Jorden if she'd adopted any new New Year's resolutions.

"Same as every year," she said. "You?"

"I'm going to make more of an effort," he said, taking a sip of champagne. He had planned on having a mimosa but changed his mind about adding the juice.

"To do what?"

Her dad shot her an obvious look: They never shared their wishes, birthday or otherwise. For atheists, they were both incredibly superstitious. "Take a raisin," he said, pointing to the bowl.

Jorden took a raisin. Her dad positioned his champagne flute near the edge of the table and told her to shoot. She took aim, fired, and missed.

"What are we playing for?" she asked.

"If it sinks, your wish comes true. If it floats, mine does."

"High stakes," said Jorden, thinking about the essay contest.

"We'll see," said her dad, pouring himself a side glass of creamy chocolate malted milk.

Jorden lobbed the raisin — it came down straight with a

plop, dead-on. It floated on the surface, then sank to the bottom. She felt guilty for winning. But just as she was about to suggest a do-over, the raisin rose slowly to the top, a host of tiny bubbles clinging to its wrinkled skin. She smiled, surprised at the twist. The raisin dropped back down. And then back up, then down, again and again, bouncing from top to bottom. The bet had two winners, and to celebrate, Jorden downed a plastic cup filled with three parts OJ, two parts champagne. Then the phone rang.

"Did you see it yet?"

"No," said Jorden. "I was waiting for you."

"I'll meet you at the Dowry in twenty minutes," said Henry, in command. Dotty's Dumpling Dowry was their favorite place for fries and shakes.

"You walking or biking?"

Henry was decisive, the color back in his cheeks. "Sailing."

He snuck out of his house through the back door, his gilded stern packed with cannons, his pirate flag flying high above the choppy suburban streets, his cutlass slashing a path as he walked. The homes on the way seemed smaller now — softer, more porous. Thanks to Jorden's training, he'd been in almost every one.

The colonial on the corner, gray with black shutters, was Mr. Finley's dream ten years ago, but now it was chipped and rickety. The place stank like mushroom. The basement was filled with bric-a-brac: old clothes, old books, old bikes with rusted gears and dented spokes. Henry never even made it upstairs.

Across the street, Mrs. Moss had quite a collection of vintage dolls and nineteenth-century wigs. Her bedroom was spotless and creepy, aromatherapy candles in the windows, a variety of empty perfume bottles displayed on a mirrored tray. Her ashtrays were overcrowded and her underwear had holes.

The Connors kept a regal study filled with choice-cut skins and furs: on the walls, on the floor, stitched into the sofa. Their kitchen had the nicest knives.

Vicky from up the block clearly enjoyed a little port after work. She wasn't too bad a painter and had very few reservations about posing for self-portraits.

Old Man Shocket had one hell of an antique train set and was deep into writing his autobiography on a Remington 5. He had a lot of memories (including a small jar of cat whiskers), many of which he stored in a hoary crib. Henry worried that he'd die before finishing.

Most people had dirty bathrooms and near-empty fridges. There were usually a variety of cheap sweets, at least one religious giveaway, a hint of solitary sexual activity, a panoply of over-the-counter pain medications and hair removal products, and everyone kept a lot of pictures. Except Professor Gall—he was an ascetic.

The only time Henry had trouble keeping his hands to himself was in the garage of a guy known around town as American Bob. Stacked high on shelves were enough fireworks to light up even the darkest soul. There were Golden Flower Fountains, Crackling Bees, Cluster Bombs, Coconut Grove Songs, Fighting Drums, Saturn Missiles, Magic Carpets, and two twenty-five-shot Howling Tigers. Henry tried convincing Jorden to let him snag a pack of Jumping Jacks, but she wouldn't budge. He took it anyway, when she wasn't looking.

* * *

Henry turned the corner, sailing fast that New Year's morning. He felt ready for the future, able-bodied and of sound mind. Then his sloop sprang a leak.

Neighbors and newspapermen arrived with cameras. Drivers stopped and rolled down their windows, dog walkers sat on curbs next to their dogs. The sirens came full circle, crowds cramped in around the cops. Henry made his way past the gawkers and wound up face-to-chest with an officer standing guard over Nika's front door.

"Is everything all right?"

The cop stood as still as an action figure.

"Did something bad happen?"

"We'll know more shortly."

"More?" said Henry. "You haven't said *anything*?"

Henry walked off toward Alton Hauser. He looked waxy up close, his hair a mass of lustrous fuzz.

"Hello, sir."

The newscaster looked at Henry as if he were a blank teleprompter. "Do you have something?" The audio guy and the makeup lady leaned in, hot for a scoop.

"No, sir," said Henry, using "sir" sarcastically, even if he didn't realize it.

"What then?" said Hauser.

"Well, that's what I was wondering. What happened in there?"

Hauser checked his lips in the camera lens, then tapped on the lavaliere microphone pinned to his lapel. "Stay tuned." He winked and walked off toward the front door.

By now the street was thronged with spectators. The house looked peaceful, if a bit haunted. It was a big old Victorian with plum-colored shutters, Palladian windows, and a cantilevered balcony. The lawn was slightly overgrown. There was a black Chrysler parked in the driveway, a snow shovel propped against a fence. White smoke drifted from the chimney's tip. Everything seemed normal, except for the smoke. The smoke seemed wrong.

Back at the Every house, Henry's father was sitting Indian-style on the kitchen floor surrounded by a bevy of aquatic hardware: jet pumps, fractionators, flow screens, beam lamps, a reservoir, a chiller, a heater, a plankton net, and the twelve-foot Kreisel tank. His stinger suit was on, his old-fashioned brass helmet snug on his head. There was no gravel, fake plants, funny pieces of coral, or decorative treasure chests—such aquascaping can harm the ultradelicate jellies.

"Henry!" yelled Dad, unaware that he'd skipped out the back. "Henry!"

Henry was on the corner of Sleet Street and Bruce Lane, waiting to intercept Jorden. She'd have to pass this way en route to the Dowry. Leaning against a mailbox tagged by Eddie, he watched the Bergers walk by, hand in hand and happy. They were newlyweds, both in their mid-thirties, in love, out for a stroll on their first day of the year. They shared everything now, even the days. Their relationship fulfilled each other's wildest dreams: An immigrant from Syria, she longed for an American husband to shop for, clean up after, and watch football games with. And hence this Dudley got his wish as well—a girl who thought he was dreamy. They noticed little things along their walk: a crow in flight, chipped paint on a fence, a heart-shaped crack in the street. But they didn't seem to hear the sirens. This made sense to Henry.

"Every!" Jorden was wearing checkered tights, skipping

down the road, kicking a juice box. She was a little tipsy from the champagne.

"What's so funny?" said Henry.

"Your face," said Jorden. For a smart girl she had a very juvenile sense of humor. Her favorite games were hide-and-go-seek and tag, and she could juggle all afternoon. She hadn't yet pierced her ears.

"Hilarious," said Henry, not in the mood. "See whose house that is?"

"Are they here to interview the winner of the essay contest?"

Henry pointed to the cops.

Jorden pointed to Hauser. "Hey, there's that guy from the news!"

"Big deal."

She tapped his cheek. "What's with the wake face?"

"Do you think this has anything to do with us?"

"Maybe she saw the paper and had a heart attack. Have you poked around?"

"Everyone's keeping quiet."

Everyone except Nika's posse, a trio of mooncalves who had just taken the area in front of the driveway. They were each without a set of individual characteristics—even their body parts seemed like accessories bought at the same store. They wore their hair high with bangs, frosted blond and crunchy from Stiff Stuff and mousse. Their ankles were fluffy with socks, their wrists ribbed with dozens of black rubber bracelets, their belly buttons shielded by a sheet of ragged mesh. Defiant with curled lips, fringed vests, and nails that glowed like shards of a stained glass window, they gave credence to triskaidekaphobics, who in this case were right to fear the number thirteen, as that was the age of these not-so-little rascals. They were clearly in the *place to be* but seemed completely unconcerned that something may have happened to their leader. Their narrow path toward world domination was about to fork, but the girls just prattled on.

"Which spelling do you like better: S-A-R-A or S-E-R-R-A?"

"There's always a backlash, everything popular goes ugly."

"Girls are the devil."

"Pretty's never ugly."

"Don't ever feel guilty for being pretty."

"I wouldn't."

"Guilt is fucking bullshit."

"Guilt is fucking ugly."

Henry listened on the sly; Jorden stared right at them. The girls noticed her and made crosses with their index fingers. Jorden batted her eyelashes. They walked away, giggling, holding their noses, and almost bumped right into Teddy, who was being carried out of the house on a stretcher, flat on his back, a few breaths shy of a toe tag.

"Silence . . . That's what Eddie Rabian heard when he walked out of the kitchen. It would be the last thing he'd ever hear. Except for his own screams."

Hauser was practicing his lines, mixing in a little ad-lib.

"I'd kill the 'scream' thing," said his writer.

"It's a bit much," said the makeup lady.

"On in five," said the PA.

The cameraman gave the countdown: "Five, four, three, two—"

"Silence," said Hauser, as if talking into a mirror. "That's what Eddie Rabian heard when he walked into the kitchen . . ."

The cameras rolled in front of a live audience.

"It was a bloodless scene, but not without tears," continued Hauser. "A brother and sister are dead. Nicole and Eddie Rabian . . . died. Teddy, Eddie's twin brother, is in critical condition at Mount Sinai Hospital. No word yet from their mother, on her way back from Fort Lauderdale where she was vacationing with a friend. This is a Greek tragedy times two."

Hauser said a few more words, expressed his condolences and his network affiliation, and flashed a hotline to call with any tips. Just as he was about to cut to a commercial, his writer shook a newspaper at him. Hauser scanned it quickly, saw the lead, and held it up for the viewers. There it was, below the fold. Victory.

"A small light in the middle of this dark tunnel," said Hauser eulogistically, the camera zooming in on the headline. "Wherever you are now, Nicole—congratulations. You've won the essay contest."

Henry had never seen a dead body. He'd never even known a dead person. Eddie and Nika were covered in sheets, but he could make out their parts underneath: a nose, an arm, five toes on a foot. It was a shock, these lumps of life—he'd expected them to flatten out, deflate, to be more . . . *life*less. Later that evening, Hauser used that very word from outside the hospital.

"The third body, that of Teddy Rabian, lifeless now as well, will be laid to rest in a joint ceremony. Whatever the protocol, whatever the formalities may be, whatever the outcome, this is a grief that will be shared by everyone in this seemingly seamless community. This is a Greek tragedy times three."

By grief he meant shock; according to autopsies, the Rabians were killed. "Poison," said the toxicologist, a stone-faced man who spoke in prose. "The killer—and there *was* a killer—wasn't particularly imaginative, choosing a classic of early twentieth-century fiction, arsenic, the dumped-on housewife's favorite bane."

Detectives found a notebook in the twins' bedroom that all but fingered Teddy as the proverbial housewife. In his hand, there were short descriptions of strychnine, arsenic, and cyanide. He'd jotted down details on dosage and a variety of case studies:

Symptoms of Poisoning

anxiety, excitement, rapid breathing, faintness, flushing, headache, nausea, drowsiness . . . In homicidal cases many of these symptoms are not seen as coma and/or death can come in as little as thirty seconds . . .

In 1982, stocks of Tylenol were spiked with cyanide. Seven "random" victims died. They never caught the killer . . . In 1911 Fredrick Seddon poisoned his lodger by soaking flypaper in his drinking water. Flypaper contains arsenic . . . In the early 1950s, Nannie Doss was convicted of murdering her five husbands, all with rat poison . . .

Doss, it seems, was the inspiration for Teddy's plan—he used her favorite recipe, but doubled up on the secret ingredient.

Nannie's Apple & Prune Pie

Approximate baking time: 45 minutes
Oven temperature: 350 degrees

INGREDIENTS

1 cup water	4 apples (sliced)
1 cup flour	1 cup dried prunes
6 tbsp. sugar	a dash of granulated sugar
½ cup butter	5 tbsp. rat poison (any old
2 eggs	brand will do)

After dinner, New Year's Eve, Teddy preheated the oven. He brought the water, butter, and sugar to a boil, then stirred in the flour and the well-beaten eggs. He greased a nine-inch pie tin, rolled out the pastry, and added the apple slices and prunes that had been soaking all day in poison. Forty-five minutes later the crust was brown and crispy, topped off with granulated sugar. Teddy called his brother and sister to the table, which was perfectly set with plates, forks, and glasses of cold whole milk. The fireplace was packed with flaming logs. There was pie for all, and seconds, too. Everyone joined the clean-plate club.

In the days and weeks that followed, Henry and Jorden watched as Nika morphed into a martyr and a poet, the essay giving her public a one-time taste of her tortured, multi-faceted mind. Everyone who'd ever even seen the girl was pressed for memories by the local media. According to the *Herald*: "Her words have become a manifesto for kids who were sick of living lies and conforming to peer pressures." The *Globe* called her an "articulator of angst" and quoted classmates saying things like "easy to talk to" and "funny" about their sorely missed chum.

The case even received national attention by way of a roundtable printed alongside Nika's essay in a glossy teen magazine. The editors gathered a cross section of girls between the ages of thirteen and fifteen to discuss what it's like *to grow up now*, and how an episode like this, while tragic, can ultimately produce a greater good.

Rachel, 14: "When you're extremely depressed, and you think about how you shouldn't be depressed because so many people have more serious problems, it just makes you *more* depressed. The hopelessness just pounds on top of you."

Meredith, 13: "When I was twelve and a half, I went through a period, like most kids do, where you want to be something you're not. And like Nika, I went into it with a bang. I just hated myself, so I became the opposite of what I was. It's not a slow process, it just hits you and you're, like, 'Wow, I can't believe I did that last night.' And then it becomes normal, like, 'Why didn't I do that last night?'"

Gina, 15: "It's an angst-filled world. And angst is trendy. It's not that Nika's angst was any better, but at least she had the courage to put it out there."

And so it went: *Nika, the Courageous. Nika, the Soothsayer. Nika, the Voice of a Generation.* The villain became an unwitting hero, and the hero kept expanding. "Nika was the darkest of holes," wrote Henry in his ledger, "but in death she was a light, and the world was brighter because of her. Even if she couldn't see it from where she was, down there, marooned with all those dirty rats and wolves and lizards."

Jorden played it cool, but you could tell she was impressed with their handiwork: "We tore down and rebuilt a person—*better*."

More than pride, though, Henry felt a deep and rousing envy. He was jealous, then inspired. He was awed by her metamorphosis—the totality of the transformation—and began to lay the groundwork for his own.

Page 1993: color-coded clear

2/1/88

It's possible. It's POSSIBLE!!!

Possible is one of those words that goes funny if you say it too much.

13

"Hi," she said.

The act itself was bigger than any words—she called, and even if she'd said nothing, the reach-out was much more than a mouthful. It took a moment for Harlan to register the pitch of her voice, the ambiguous accent. He'd seen her just over a week ago, at Henry's funeral, but they'd barely spoken. She'd stayed at a hotel. Besides, he was drunk now. And not just drunk, he'd taken to spiking his gin with Fiorinal.

"Hi," he said, clearing his throat, sitting up on the sofa.

"How've you been?" Hannah had a way of transcending the requisite. Her "how've you beens" weren't space fillers; her "I miss yous" and her "thank yous" and her "sorrys" were far from perfunctory. One watched in awe as she paid a condolence call, or admitted she was wrong, or told a friend she felt happy they'd succeeded. But she wouldn't rise for just any occasion. Sometimes she'd stay quiet. Like when she and Harlan were at the tail end of their patience and there was nothing left between them but packed boxes and dead space and loss. Her quiets were the worst.

"Okay," he said, blood swerving through his veins.

"I thought of you tonight."

"Yeah?"

"Termites aren't ants," she said.

"Sorry?"

"They're part of the cockroach family."

Harlan rubbed his eyes.

"Remember how you'd call me 'termite' when you were angry? How you'd say I'd be better off in my terrarium, with my termites, and I'd say 'termites aren't ants,' and you'd say 'same difference'?"

"I remember," said Harlan.

"Well, termites aren't related to ants." She left a space for him to speak, but he didn't. "This whole time I thought they were related, but tonight I found out they're not. They're related to cockroaches."

"Cockroaches," said Harlan.

"I also learned that ants have the largest brains in proportion to their bodies."

"You always said they were smarter than us."

"The biggest brain of *any* animal, not just insects. But they're only brainy when part of a community. Alone, they're just about useless. Like when they're foraging, looking for food, they follow a chemical trail left by their sisters. If you painted a circle of that chemical, and dropped a single ant on it, she'd walk in circles until she starved to death. They *need* each other."

In the beginning, Harlan loved it when she got excited about things like bug brains. "I almost just called you 'Honey,'" he said.

"Old habits—"

"I was gonna start my sentence with 'Honey.'"

"And what would I have said?"

"I don't know."

"I had habits, too, didn't I? Pet names, pet peeves . . ."

"You had a lot of pets," he said.

"How's the reading going?" She was referring to the ledger; Henry often discussed its contents with her over the phone.

"Did you know Jorden's father was bulimic?"

"Yes," said Hannah.

"Henry knew all about the polyps I tried to have sent to him from Australia. He called *every*one—Customs, UPS, FedEx, the Department of Fish and Wildlife. I never knew he knew." Harlan seemed proud of his son. "I miss him."

"Yes," she said. "Me too."

Harlan downed his gin. "I mice you, Hannah."

One night, during their seemingly blissful stage, he decided that "miss" didn't adequately describe how he felt when they were apart. "People miss their cats," he'd said. "They miss red meat. We need a stronger word."

Now she smiled warmly. He felt it all the way from the Netherlands. "I mice you, too."

14

A line in Henry's ledger read: "High school is an experimental time." But he'd crossed out "experimental" and above it wrote "probationary." Then he wrote: "I'm sick of being undecided. I need to join forces with something." This was written in the spring of his freshman year, just before he died.

In Henry's high school there was a central hallway called the Cord, an extra-wide artery that ran from one end of the building to the other. Along this corridor were "houses"—six in all, one after the next. They were separated by walls, distinguished by color, each with their own set of lockers and a common room invariably called the Commons. Students were randomly assigned a house, but it rarely stuck, the sum and substance of their would-be personas determining where they'd hang their coats.

First up were the red walls and lockers, Bacon House, where combat boots and skateboards mixed with "art fags" and stylized nerds. Then came purple, Riley House, the rich kids, khaki and sockless and stoned. Next was Palmer House, light blue, for "big-hairs" who worked on cars and liked tight pants and heavy metal. Adams House was hunter green, the place where younger jocks held court among the girls who cheered them on. Eventually they'd get to Beals, light green, the house their older brothers warned them to steer clear of, or catch a playful beating. And finally there was Barry, the last house on the left, the bright yellow home for the genuinely alternative: the handicapped. Henry hoped that by graduation he'd have hung his coat in all of them.

On the first day of school, though, he leaned toward Bacon. It was closest to the front door, and there was a free red locker next to Jorden's, who was actually assigned to be there. They hadn't spoken all summer, since she found out about the Jumping Jacks he'd stolen from American Bob. She didn't *find out* exactly — Henry showed them to her one night after they'd split a flask of Southern Comfort on the golf course of a restricted country club. He lit one off and she said, "Cool," and then he stammered when asked, "Where'd you get 'em?" She was quick to his fib and took off, pissed.

Page 2015: color-coded purple

9/3/88

It's not like I stole the pie from her windowsill, it was a goddamn pack of Jumping Jacks! But I get it, I do — it's not what you steal, it's the fact that you stole. More important, in this case, I broke our deal. I know that, and I'm sorry, but I think Jorden might be taking it too far. It's not, as she said, "a symptom of a greater, latent evil." We haven't spoken all summer. Are all women like this?

Dad says women are like bruises: tender, painful, colorful, and they go away eventually. But he's talking about women who are more than friends. He says Jorden might have more-than-friends feelings for me and that's why she's acting so crazy. I don't think so. I really don't. Truth is, he says, girls care a lot less about looks.

Over the summer Jorden had turned into a woman. She stood five feet six with a swing in her hips; her hair was long and wild, as if she'd just stepped off a speedboat after a day in the sun. Her eyes had gone from saucers to almonds, a budding cynicism scrunching the lids into a "yeah, right" squint. Her outfits went from sloppy to sharp—not that she was fashionable. She wasn't. She didn't believe in fashion. And she didn't need any breast jam.

"I think my sentence is up," said Henry, in front of his red locker.

Jorden grabbed her math book; she was late.

"Hell*o-oh!*" he said, pushing his face close to hers. She was wearing perfume and lip-gloss. She never used to wear perfume and lip-gloss. Henry noticed these things. He never used to notice these things.

"Hi," she said, slamming the locker, walking off.

His eyes trailed her butt as she walked.

Gimmel was standing there and heard the whole thing. "She wants you," she said.

"I don't think so," said Henry.

Mope Pope and Gimmel were sophomores. They shared a red locker next to Henry's. Gimmel was taller with bigger feet, her hair less than half an inch long beneath her trademark painter's cap. Mope Pope was lean, aloof, his small head lost beneath a well-conditioned mane of black hair. On the back of his leather jacket he'd written "The Eternal" in Wite-Out. Straight-edge by creed, they didn't smoke or drink, but they kissed like addicts—like they needed to. It made Henry jeal-

ous. He wanted to be addicted to something. He'd tried ciga-
rettes, coffee, a variety of liquor, pot, whip-its—enjoyed them
all—but couldn't imagine needing them. He wanted to need.

"Believe me," said Gimmel. "She wants you."

"That's the first thing she's said to me in months."

"Why else would she care so much?"

"She doesn't care at all. She *hates* me."

"You let her down," said Gimmel.

"Yes," said Henry.

"She must've held you pretty high."

"We held each other."

"I'm Gimmel," she said, holding out her hand that was
covered with blue ink doodles.

"Henry Every," he said.

"If you need anything, just knock." She knocked on her
locker and walked off toward Mope Pope, who was watching
the exchange from afar. They French kissed and strolled
down the hall. Just before reaching the exit, Mope Pope
pulled up his collar and looked back over his shoulder at
Henry.

During the summer Henry had honed his browsing skills, cali-
brating his scopes and training them on a more targeted
swath of the public. As his father sank deeper into the Cnidarian netherworld, Henry spent more time away from home.
He became an expert at reconnaissance, marking pertinent
"cases" and studying them on the street, in the grocery store,
taking note of their public face so he could later stack it up
against the private. Gone were the days of roaming through
parallel white-flight suburbs with hopes of stumbling into relevant lives.

9/8/88

I've been taking the trolley all over town. Sometimes I'll see someone who I think is worth browsing. A cripple, a Negro, a Krishna, a queer. An albino. Maybe a bum or a midget. I'll see them sitting down or walking around and I'll just follow them for a little while, usually not for more than a few hours. Sometimes I'll even trail squirrels or insects, but I don't like to run.

Like last Wednesday, I was in a video store in the Combat Zone and over in the corner I saw this very obese man steal two porno-movie boxes. Just the boxes. He put them in a gym bag. It looked funny, this fat man with a gym bag. Then he went into a pet store, bought fish food and a fly swatter, stopped to talk to a man on the street with an electric guitar, showed him the fly swatter, then went home to an apartment building. I followed him into the building (he held the door for me), passed him on the stairs, then came back down and pressed my ear against his door. He growled at a woman who grunted back, but they were foreign so I couldn't understand. It doesn't last very long if you can't understand.

Yesterday was better. I found a four-bedroom house in Roxbury with tinfoil over the unlocked windows. In the backyard was this crappy wooden barrel filled with rainwater. Inside there were all sorts of animals, over a hundred, most of them in cages, most of them pretty sick looking. Some of them were definitely dead. It reeked like piss and shit and ammonia. In every room there were cages and cages lined up in neat rows. There were tons of cats and dogs, about twenty birds, ten hamsters, a bunch of lizards, ferrets, a dozen rabbits, some rats and gerbils, eight chinchillas, a turtle, and a couple of fish.

There were no pictures of people anywhere. It smelled so bad I thought I would puke.

Before I left, I opened all the cages. I said things like "Come on, boy!" and "Here, girl!" and "You're free!" But it was no use. They just stayed put. They didn't want to leave.

I've been thinking a lot about why those animals didn't want to leave and about who trapped them in the first place. I think about putting *them* in a filthy cage and feeding them rainwater. I think about how lots of times I feel caged. All I know is I'd never want to be caged so long that if someone tried to free me I'd just stay put.

15

Page 2089: color-coded clear

11/14/88

Today Jorden gave me a present, even though we still haven't spoken. It was a pretty heavy box wrapped in the movie section of the newspaper. She left it in front of my locker, no card. Gimmel was standing right next to me when I opened it. The box was filled with dirt. Very suspenseful. "What did you do now?" she asked. I shrugged. She touched the dirt and smelled her fingers. I patted the surface then took a breath and stuck my hand in all the way. I was prepared for the worst — fangs, goo — even to be sucked into another dimension. What I found was bigger than anything. Buried inside was a small hatchet. It took me a second to catch the symbolism.

Tomorrow I leave for New York to see my grandmother Lulu, my dad's mom. We don't have any other names for her like Nanna or Grammy or Bubbe — everyone just calls her Lulu. Dad calls her Grand Exalted Ruler on account of her heavy-handed ways. She and Mom get along real well, they still talk on the phone a lot, but Dad's not close with her so

I'm not either. They don't hate each other or anything — there wasn't some big blowup — they just don't really like each other. They clash, Mom says. I've actually only seen Lulu like five times in my whole life, and one of those times I was only a week old so it doesn't really count.

Henry's mother never asked favors of friends. Only slightly easier for her was asking one of a family member. She was best at *doing* favors, and on this particular occasion the recipient was her mother-in-law. Lulu's seventy-fifth elementary school reunion was taking place over Thanksgiving weekend in New York City, where she lived. Everyone who ever went to the school was invited. One of the oldest living alumni, Lulu was eager to go, but not by herself. She wanted a date. "Grandsons are like celebrities," Mom told Henry. Considering the environment at home — jellies, jellies, jellies — he was more than happy to offer his arm.

Henry thought of New York in comic book terms: hyperreal, cabalistic, neon, and mean. He pictured it literally buzzing, filled with damsels and apes, rainbow people and underground tunnels, modern-day pirates and robber barons. The ladies of Fifth Avenue were highbrow and sassy under lavish hats, their husbands rich as pharaohs. It was an apt description of Lulu, only she didn't need anyone else's money.

Born on the cusp of the century, Lulu's father was a Russian Jew named Becker who arrived at Ellis Island just after Germany torpedoed the *Lusitania*. He took a room in a tumbledown boarding house and fell hard for the aproned girl who changed his sheets. They were both fifteen. Two months later, they were married. She kept her job but moved into his room. A year later Lulu was born, and in her honor, the entrepreneurial immigrant borrowed one hundred dollars to buy a machine he used to cut the tongues for leather shoes. Little Lulu would help her mom with the linen, but by the time she was seven her father was walking around in suede spats. He owned three shoe factories, two touring cars, and the boarding house in which Lulu was conceived. The women in his life never again changed anyone else's sheets, not even their own.

At twenty-three, Lulu married a saint from the old neighborhood who, according to him, discovered the secret to comedy: He invented the laugh track in 1948. He wasn't *really* a saint — he was a gizmo guy — but that's what people said of him. Thirty years after unveiling his revolutionary Laff Box, the old man died smiling in his sleep. Lulu thought it only right to remain a "one-fella gal," but the death hit her particularly hard, especially at night. She sulked. She played solitaire. She took tranquilizers. Occasionally she'd break the silence with a blast of canned laughter, but the effect was one of mockery, not levity. She stowed the machine in a closet.

Eventually Lulu hired a housekeeper, a hearty Cuban from Spanish Harlem's East River housing projects. A former cook in a kosher deli, her specialty was breakfast meats — kippered salmon, corned beef hash — and a combo dish she called "payalaya" (a cross between paella and jambalaya). They lived together in an imposing, marble-trimmed townhouse in Greenwich Village.

For a while Lulu kept her distance and referred to her housemate only as "You," partly because of an early incident involving a twenty-dollar bill. Lulu kept $261 on her desk in an antique silent butler (a gift from her husband). One day she counted: $241. She fanned the money on the desk, leaving a conspicuous space for the missing bill. The following day, the fan was complete. It was never spoken of, and it never happened again. Eventually Lulu took to calling her housemate "Papi," the Spanish term of endearment for both fathers and sons.

It was a peculiar union. Lulu, eighty-five, was self-consciously ladylike; Papi, twenty-three, cussed like a stick-up kid. Lulu romanticized her childhood; Papi wanted nothing more than to trade hers in. Lulu dropped her pennies in the street so that finders could keep the luck; Papi saved hers in a jar. The one thing they had in common was a taste for sweet liquor, and, eventually, a devotion to each other—though you'd never know it by the way they spoke.

"Don't *make* me come in there," said Papi, dressed like a hooker, standing outside Lulu's bedroom on a Saturday night. Lulu had stolen her trusty condoms as a deterrent. "Umma give you three counts—after that you gon' feel the thump."

"That dress is from *hun*ger," said Lulu, safe behind the bolt. "Haven't you anything decent?"

Papi checked herself out, briefly second-guessing the wraparound sheet that barely covered her breasts. Like a rebel daughter, deep down she sought Lulu's approval. "Who's up to look decent? I look *good*."

"Your taste is in your *mouth*," said Lulu.

In their less combative moments Papi grabbed her mix tapes and the women ascended to the roof garden and drank. It was Papi's favorite part of the house. From the west side you could see right into the Hudson River. "I'm a different person up here," Papi would say, uncharacteristically relaxed. "It's like being in a better body."

Lulu would get tipsy and gush about her childhood, her father, but mostly her husband.

"How well you know a man after all those years?" asked Papi.

"Like an x-ray," said Lulu, and she'd share some of the darker fissures. Their dry spells, her box full of dishes that broke during fights, the time he used a World War II air raid siren to drown out her niggling. Or the fact that, after he died, she found out he was seven years older than he'd said, and that he took mind-boggling pains to forever hide his false teeth. "Everyone has their shtick," she'd say.

Papi told Lulu how, as a girl, she got used to the needles in the stairways and the hungry weeks filled with nothing but rice and beans and watered-down milk. She told her about the leaky ceiling pipes, and how she'd have to sit on the toilet with an umbrella. Born to an abusive teenager, she was the eldest of three: always a *madre*, never a *mamita*. When she'd look at Lulu—her gray mane dyed young, her skin stretched over old bones—she wavered between her primal instincts: she wanted to take care of her like a child and at the same time crawl inside her stomach.

"I got real good at impressions," said Papi. "I could do *any-*one. Anything to escape."

"What did you want to be?" said Lulu.

Papi shrugged. "Like you, I guess."

Sometimes, after they were good and drunk, they'd braid each other's hair.

In the garden on the Sunday before Thanksgiving, Lulu told Papi about a boy named Henry who was coming to stay with them for a couple of days.

"With *us*?"

"Yes," said Lulu.

"Never heard you talk of no grandson."

"What you've never heard could fill an ocean."

"What's his name then?"

Lulu motioned for Papi to pour more sangria. She did, right to the brim. "Henry," said Lulu. "He's not *really* my grandson."

Papi sensed a problem she could relate to. "Mystery pop?"

Lulu shook her head. "My son's boy."

"Foster?"

"My son has a syndrome."

"He droopy-eyed?"

"Kartagener's syndrome. It's a genetic disorder." Lulu put her index finger to her lips. "It's a secret."

Papi whispered. "He don't know he's sick?"

"He isn't sick."

Papi scrunched up her wide nose and said, "Deformed?"

Lulu shook her head and went on to explain that, aside from sterility, one of the side effects is *situs inversus* — mixed-up organs. "His heart, his liver, his spleen — they're all on the wrong side. Not the *wrong* side — the *other* side. They're inverted." She defined words like *dextrocardia: dextro* = right, *cardia* = heart. Her son's heart was slightly to the right, instead of where it should be, *levocardia,* slightly to the left. *Situs inversus,* she said — sides switched.

"What about his face?" asked Papi. "Ears? Nose?"

"Handsome. Normal. You wouldn't know except to look inside."

"Why he don't know then?"

"We never told him," said Lulu. "Doctor said it might make him feel freakish. We meant to, eventually, in time — but then time passed and it was too late. He had a son. Well, so to speak."

"So whose kid is this Henry?"

"His mother's," said Lulu. "Wonderful girl. With her first husband, a real *bum*. He died just after she got pregnant, just after the honeymoon."

Papi bugged her eyes as if she'd just caught the final twist in a soap opera.

"Nobody knows," warned Lulu.

"Except you," said Papi.

"And his mother," said Lulu.

Papi beamed; she felt like a real family member. "And now me."

16

By Thanksgiving the steep part of puberty had leveled off. Puffy tufts of hair had sprouted in all the right places, Henry's voice turned coarser, and almost all of his thoughts were rooted in the base desire to lay naked with his female classmates—and their sisters, their cousins, and sometimes even their mothers. There were books in the attic—medical texts, a short stack of *Playboys*—which Henry had successfully used to reverse all the damage from that myth-ridden old Cyclopedia. He knew well that masturbation and amorous dreams produced no deleterious effects whatsoever, and he used this newfound wisdom to explore his up-and-coming proclivities. New York, he hoped, would offer some practical counterpoints, a corporal crack at rousing the gametes and zygotes and sperm he'd been reading all about. If nothing else, he heard there were peep shows.

Henry arrived with a hanging bag at noon via taxi on the corner of Fifth Avenue and Ninth Street. The doorman stared at him over the edge of his newspaper. He was a stocky, dark-skinned man who wore ankle weights under his slacks. Most Village townhouses didn't have doormen, but Lulu thought it important to maintain a *baleboss* of the house. She and Papi lived on the second floor; the man lived on the ground floor.

"You must be the Henry," he said—Calvin, according to his nametag.

"I don't know if I'm *the* Henry."

Calvin picked up the phone to announce the visitor.

Henry dropped his bag. "Can I ask you a question?"

"Yes," said Calvin, hanging up the phone.

On the train ride Henry had made an incomplete list of minorities and subcultures that he split into three categories: "Born Into," "Joined," and "Other." Category 1 included those defined by, say, race or birth defects like blindness, deafness, and albinism. Category 2 contained cults and specialty groups like the Navy SEALS and the clergy. And Category 3, marked by asterisks, was for "vagaries and accidents"—convicts, religious types, and victims of extreme illness or atrocity —for example, a person who became a paraplegic.

"What nationality are you?" asked Henry.

"I am Latino."

"From what part of the world?"

"Puerto Rico."

Henry loved how natives pronounced their countries. "I've never been to *Puerto Rico* but it seems quite beautiful. I've seen the ads for *Puerto Rico* on the *télévisión*."

"For the tourism, yes."

"Is Latino the same as Hispanic?"

Calvin thought for a moment. "I no sure."

"Do you like being Latino? And/or Hispanic?"

"Oh, I like it *very* much."

"You feel at home being Latino/Hispanic. You think it suits you."

"Oh, yes."

"Did you ever want to be anything else?"

"Else?"

"Something different. Other than Latino. Or Hispanic."

"Ah." Calvin rose a few inches on his tiptoes. "I wish to be taller."

Henry smiled and offered Calvin a piece of gum. Calvin declined, saying it was "unlawful" to chew at work. Henry insisted he take a piece for later and Calvin put the gum in his pocket.

"It's okay now?" he said, picking up the receiver. "I announce your presence?"

Henry nodded. He'd never before had his presence announced. It made him feel like a fraud.

The door at the top of the wraparound stairs was unlocked but not open. Henry took this as a sign to enter. Once inside, he was taken aback by the darkness. Not just the lack of light, but the shades of the furnishings, the stain of the wood. Deep red and mahogany, hunter green and coal. There was a fireplace filled with candles and an antique oven filled with books. Henry noticed a collection of shoes lined up in pairs by the door. He took his off as well. There was a small pile of rolled-up tissues on the floor by a black-and-white TV with a VCR balanced on top of it. As Henry stood and wondered what substance was holding the tissues together, he was greeted.

"Knock much?" said Papi, standing barefoot in a pair of black pajamas.

"It was open," said Henry, embarrassed. "Sorry." He turned and began putting his shoes back on.

"Who's there?" called a voice from beyond: Lulu's.

"No one," said Papi, and then, whispering to Henry, "Well, come on then."

Again he took off his shoes. It was now well after noon but the place had an early morning vibe. Henry was beginning to feel like the unwanted rooster.

"Wipe your feet," said Papi.

Henry looked at his shoes, confused.

"Never mind," she said, easing into the high-backed red master chair. "Have a seat."

Henry sat on the sofa. Papi slipped a skinny ring off her index toe then pushed it back on. She seemed very at home in the red chair, as if she longed to one day be its rightful sitter. "Let me see your fingers."

Henry held out his hands, tips up, flat against the air.

She nodded approvingly. "You dirty?"

"Messy?"

"Are you *clean?*"

"Like a duck," said Henry, realizing with whom he was speaking—the copper-haired keeper his mother told him about.

"*Nuh*-uh," said Papi, shaking her head. "We don't like birds."

"You're Hispanic, right?"

"American," said Papi, tough.

"What's the difference between Hispanic and Latino?"

Lulu appeared from the back bedroom, her face made up, perfumed. Papi immediately sprang out of the chair and stood a few inches behind her boss.

"Henry," said Lulu, her hands outstretched. "You made it."

Instead of hugging her, he awkwardly shook both her hands. "Hi, Lulu."

"I appreciate your coming to be my date."

"It's my first real date, actually."

"Good thing you're not related," said Papi, under her breath.

"This is Papi," said Lulu, stone-faced. "She's a dummy."

"Now that ain't *even* true."

"It's not a lie, either."

Henry brought his only formal outfit to wear for the special occasion; it had been hanging in his closet for as long as he could remember, upped in size about every eighteen months. It was his only real connection to Lulu. She had a charge card at Brooks Brothers and insisted on being the one to keep him properly clothed.

On the evening of the school reunion, Henry stood waiting for his date in the living room, wearing gray wool gabardine slacks, a navy blazer with gold buttons, a cordovan leather belt, a light blue oxford with button-down collar, and cordovan penny loafers, slightly scuffed. It was as much of a costume as any he'd worn on Halloween.

Lulu came out sparkling, her green gown fresh from the department store. The ensemble had likely been planned for months, right down to the rhinestone barrettes. Papi trailed her, assessing. They both treated dress-up nights very seriously.

"Well, don't you look like a little gentleman," said Lulu.

"You look very nice, too," said Henry. "I like that big pin." She was wearing her mother's brooch, a hand-painted ivory mold of a pretty girl's face trimmed in twenty-four-karat gold. On her middle finger was a giant yellow plastic ring. She bought it for a quarter in a supermarket vending machine because it looked "very young." She was always wearing something young, as if the accessory somehow created a diversion. She kept such jewelry in the bottom drawer of an old hope chest, on top of which was a prescription for Premarin.

"She shoulda worn the *other* shoes," said Papi.

"Shoo," said Lulu, as if waving at a horsefly.

Papi told Henry, "She's hoping her first boyfriend shows up. She ain't seen him in forever."

"See you later, dummy," said Lulu, hooking Henry's arm and leading him toward the door. Lulu hated goodbyes — never used the word. She'd always just say "see you later."

The Ettinger School began as an experiment, conceived of in 1903 by a young woman from Fieldston, New York, who would eventually become known as the matriarch of progressive education. She'd later place the germ of inspiration at Kitty Hawk, North Carolina, where she stood in awe as the Wright Brothers first took flight. Six years later, among blossoming English apple trees, she met a high-flying architect who said she was the needle in the haystack and twice as sharp. In addition to her hand in marriage, he received nine acres of land as her dowry, on which the newlyweds sketched out their dreams. Backed by a wealthy and childless man called Ettinger, they built a school for children in kindergarten through sixth grade in the residential style of the northwestern Bronx. There would be a sandbox in the back, a wrought-iron jungle gym, and a collection of pear trees, just fine for climbing in your knickers.

At the time, many in the community thought the new school far too loose a place to learn. Instead of sitting in neat rows, the children were given movable desks that could be arranged in different configurations. Gym was coed, the walls were filled with colorful murals, and cursive writing was left off the lesson plan. Students were encouraged to study in groups, and no one had to raise their hands to talk. By the late 1930s, Ettinger kids had the highest IQs in the city.

"It's where I got the big mouth I spent the rest of my life shutting," said Lulu, sitting at a table in the alumni lounge with a few of her old cronies: Efram Katz, her first boyfriend; Efram's buddy Billy Basker (who was always referred to by his full name) and his mousy wife, Phyllis; and Efram's twin sister, Sylvia, a lively blond *yente* in Kabuki-like makeup who had done very well on the inheritance circuit. They were the royalty of the day, the only ones there from Day One.

"She was always into mischief, this one," recalled Efram, recently divorced from his third wife and dressed in a freshly starched shirt, tie, and hearing aid. "You always knew when Lulu was in school."

"I did receive the prize for posture," said Lulu coyly.

"And a couple McKenzie milkshakes!" said Billy Basker, retired now from the textile business. Miss McKenzie was their fourth grade teacher who was famous for her "milkshakes," named for her tendency to shake a student by the shoulders when they acted up.

"She used to stink out loud," said Sylvia, behind dark, fashionable glasses. "Never took a bath."

Henry was enjoying himself. He kept relatively quiet, admiring the durability of human relationships even as the bodies turned fragile. He thought of his high school and wondered in which color lockers these old folks would have hung their coats. There was the requisite talk of So-and-so's diverticulitis, the prednisone that So-and-so's been taking, and how So-and-so is overweight and wakes up with the shakes. But overall it was a very inviting group of people. "It's as much a private club as any, these senior citizens," Henry later wrote in his ledger. "A very exclusive, federally sanctioned club. One we'll all get into, sure, if we make it, but there's no sneaking in, no sponsoring your buddy. You just have to wait."

"'*Course* things were better back then," Efram told Henry, sipping a Dewar's and water. "It was nice living in those days. We were all-American kids. We played ball. Took our sleds to the hills. We didn't fool around with girls 'cause we didn't know what they were. You could go anywhere you wanted; the doors were always unlocked. It was a much freer atmosphere. Now you're always looking over your shoulder."

"We used to collect the golf balls from the eighth hole of the Commonwealth Country Club," said Billy Basker, whose wife hadn't gone to Ettinger and seemed incredibly bored, slouched in a chair, letting out the occasional sigh. Henry hated unjustified sighs. There were sighs that were perfectly justified, he thought, but the unjustified ones were the worst. "Irving Berlin came to play golf there once and a friend of mine jumped on his cart to say hello to him!"

"That wasn't Irving Berlin, it was Gene Greene," said Sylvia. She and Billy Basker had once messed around in the rumble seat of her old man's Packard, but it was never spoken of in front of Phyllis.

"Gene Greene?" said Billy Basker.

"King of the Bungaloos," said Sylvia, citing his 1911 hit.

"Ring of *what?*" said Efram, cupping his bad ear.

"Would anyone like anything from the food table?" said Henry. "I'm going to get some cookies."

"Those cookies are *wonderful*," said Lulu.

"I'll have a cookie," said Phyllis. "Oatmeal raisin."

Henry mock sighed and walked over to the table. He picked up a couple oatmeal raisins. A rich-looking lady from the class of '39 noticed that his loafers matched his belt and asked if he was an Ettinger boy.

"No," said Henry. "I'm here with my grandmother. She was here in 1913."

"Oh? What's her name?"

"Lulu Every," said Henry, realizing he didn't know her maiden name.

The lady squinted, shrugged. "Come, I want you to meet someone." She was apparently there with her granddaughter, who also went to Ettinger, class of '83. "She's a little phantom, always disappearing. Stand on that chair, will you? Tell me if you see a pretty phantom."

Henry reluctantly mounted the chair. As soon as he started scanning the room his eyes met Lulu's. She frowned, so he stepped down. "I'm sure she'll materialize," said Henry, and walked back toward the old people, who were talking about marriage.

"If you marry for money, you earn every goddamn penny," said Efram. "Rich girls are tougher."

"All depends," said Lulu. "It all depends who you marry. There are plenty of rich girls who are very nice."

"And how!" said Billy Basker, self-consciously clutching Phyllis's bejeweled hand.

"You live a better *life* when you marry a rich girl," said Phyllis. "The poor girls, they're tough. They want everything they never had."

"But the rich girls, they want everything they're accustomed to," said Billy Basker. "If they get it, big deal. And if they don't—*whoah, boy!*"

Phyllis pulled her hand away.

Lulu said to Henry, "It's just as easy to fall in love with a rich girl as it is with a poor girl. Remember that. Marry for love, but remember that."

"Love doesn't go away," said Efram. "Not real love."

"Bull!" said Sylvia. "When there's no bread on the table, love flies out the window. And then you have one baby, then *another* baby. Come on, don't give me that, Efram. You don't think that. You don't know."

"No, *you* know. I like the way women tell me. Tell *me*— Efram Katz—about marrying rich girls and poor girls. Like *they* know." Efram looked at Henry. "There's an old saying: A man will chase a woman until she catches him. Until *she* catches *him*."

"Oh sure," said Sylvia, implying just the opposite.

"A man got all the goddamn sex he wants if he's single," said Efram. "What the hell's he wanna get married for?"

"*Unless*," said Lulu.

"Unless you fall in love," said Efram. "If you *really fall in love*. Otherwise—" He shrugged, then stood up. "I'm going to the john." He leaned down and whispered to Henry, "When you get older you have to go to the john a lot more."

While Efram was gone the rich-looking lady came over and stood above the table for a moment. She apparently recognized the Baskers. "Phyllis?!" she said.

Phyllis turned around. "Evelyn?!"

They knew each other from the country club. Phyllis and Evelyn played bridge together; Billy Basker occasionally played golf with Evelyn's ex-husband.

"Billy Basker?!" said Evelyn. "I didn't know you went to Ettinger!"

"Ett-in-ger!" He began singing the school song. "It's number one in New York, Ett-in-ger . . ." Then Lulu joined in, then Evelyn, then Sylvia. Pretty soon the entire place erupted, seventy-five years' worth of progressively educated voices. Phyllis hunched and rolled her eyes.

> We live, we love, we learn
> We have no fear
> The buck starts here
> We are the children!
> Chug-ah, chug-ah
> We're the future!
> Chug-ah, chug-ah
> And we'll see you all at Ettinger next year!
> Oh yes, we'll see you all
> At Ett . . . in . . . ger . . . next . . . yeeeaaar!

They all laughed, united. Then Evelyn noticed Henry at the table. "You!"

Henry cocked his eyebrows.

"My lookout man!"

"Hi," said Henry.

"How old is he?" Evelyn asked Lulu. "He's adorable."

Lulu looked to Henry for help. "Fifteen," he said.

"Good!" said Evelyn, looking around the room.

Henry felt like a frog in formaldehyde. He politely excused himself.

"Where are you going?" asked Evelyn.

"To the john," whispered Henry. "When you get older you have to go a lot more."

He pushed through the large, green doors as if exiting a dream. Someone had a fire going outside. He reminded himself where he was, *who* he was, and how long it would be before his senior citizenship kicked in. He strolled, whistling, hands in his pockets like a retiree, just like he'd done in grade school. "I've a long way to go," he thought.

Around the corner from the school were a variety of food carts selling Sno-Kones, fried dough, kielbasa, hot dogs. Henry approached the hot dog stand. The girl in front of him ordered a hot dog with everything—*hold the hot dog*. She turned, bun in hand, and stood face-to-face with Henry: "With all that stuff on there you can't even tell it's missing."

It was remarkable—she looked just like the girl on Lulu's brooch. Henry contemplated her symmetrical face, her elegant neck, then skipped down to her feet, her shins, her thighs, her waist, and as he made his way past her stomach, over her developed breasts, he noticed that her right arm came up short. There were biceps, triceps, elbows, forearms, but she was missing her right hand. The limb thinned out and quit just short of her wrist. She kept it close to her body, out of plain sight; had he not been looking so thoroughly he would have missed it. Henry stared as if from behind a one-way mirror. She stared back. "Wanna bite?"

There were moments that Henry knew would later be classified in his ledger as "world-changing." This surpassed them all. He instinctively leaned in and took a bite of her hot dog, his arms hanging limp in their sockets. The stranger wiped his mouth with her napkin. His first thought was to ask if he could have it as a souvenir. He felt unusual, weightless and giddy, as if he'd been spinning on the lawn for hours. It was too much. He dug deep for an anchor—the *Great Ovations*, Moo's severed head. *Could she even clap?* He thought of the bike rack and the waves crashing the hull of Long Ben's sloop. Of Nika and the turtle-man. But nothing. He was on his own.

"Good," she said abstractly, taking a bite from where he had taken a bite.

She could have chosen the other end — she could've, but she didn't. She bit right where I bit. Then swallowed. He pictured himself swimming in her stomach.

"What's your name?" he mustered.

"Benna." She took the final bite and put out her left hand. She was wearing nail polish. Henry shook her hand and wondered how she painted her nails. How she buttoned her shirt, how she cut her steak.

"Are you a New Yorker?" he said, trying to place this otherworldly creature in some sort of earthly context.

She nodded, her mouth full.

"You live up here?"

"Uh-uh." She pointed south with her only thumb. "Down there. You?"

"Visiting grandma," he said.

"I'm with mine, too. Ettinger?"

"Yeah!"

"Me too! Mine's been hawking me all night."

"Yeah, this lady's been —" Henry stopped short, noticing the resemblance. Benna basketball-shot the napkin at a trash can. She missed. Henry justifiably sighed. "So *you're* the pretty phantom."

As she bent over to pick up the napkin the fire alarm rang out from the school. Like a crime-fighting duo Henry and Benna charged headlong into the bedlam. He held the door for her on the way in. She noticed and said, "Thanks," the peal of the bell getting louder with each ding. The younger alumni were quick to gather their things, but the old people in the lounge stayed put, as if they were fireproof.

"It'll stop," said Sylvia.

"These things always stop," said Billy Basker.

"And so what if it doesn't?" said Lulu.

Henry and Benna rushed over to the table. Lulu and Evelyn were talking to each other about fertilizer, totally oblivious to the possibility of impending doom. They didn't even see Henry and Benna walk in. Efram returned from the john, his beige hearing aid in his hand.

"Do you people hear a ringing?" he asked, tapping the device, wiggling his finger in his ear. "I think this thing is busted."

Henry and Benna looked at each other and laughed — really laughed — so loud that it drowned out all the cookies and the clamor and Henry's time-flying desire to become a senior citizen. Whatever he was right then, in that very moment — that's what he wanted to be.

Later it came out that the alarm had been pulled. People cast their eyes on the clowns of the past, mostly on Sheppy Kussel, class of '38, who once famously poured a pailful of sugar in Miss McKenzie's gas tank. "Musta been ol' Shep," they said.

But they were wrong. It was Billy Basker's bored and mousy wife.

17

Page 2096: color-coded blue

11/24/88

I walked Benna to her hotel, the Alcazar, on Fifth. Her father owns it so she lives there — has her own room and everything. In the lobby she asked me if I knew how to crack my knuckles. I said no and she said, "Come up, I'll show you." I told her I had twice as many knuckles as she did and that it might take a while. I thought that was pretty suave, you know, putting it right out there instead of looking away. I guess she agreed because we didn't come down until the following night. Truth is, I wouldn't have come down at all. I ended up feeling a little bad, though, because Lulu called the cops and the hospitals. She was really worried, thought I might have been abducted or taken hostage or something. And she wasn't far off, I tell you, not far off at all.

Papi said she looked for me by doing something called *darle coco al santo,* which means "give the coconut to the saint." Under a waxing moon she cracked open a coconut so she could read its meat. She says she's a Santera. She has wooden witch pegs nailed into her floor. She even keeps a black rag doll on her dresser and a jar of water under her bed to dissolve evil spirits. She changes the water every twenty-four hours. Anyway, she cracked the coconut into four pieces, dropped them on the floor, and by the pattern was able to tell that I was okay. Lulu appreciated the effort but wasn't convinced — she called the whole practice *tsedrayt*. I could tell she was scared because she hugged me tight and angry when I walked in the door.

She's right, of course, I should've called, and I would've if all the earth, air, water, fire, and certainly the phones of the world hadn't seemed so meaningless in comparison to the hours I spent in that room. It's amazing how simple it all is. Me and a girl in a room. That's it, that's everything. It was definitely a room (with four walls, a floor, a ceiling) but I hesitate to include Benna in such a common classification — there are like three *billion* girls in the world. No, Benna is something else, something *other*. Me, I'm just lucky. Which is its own form of other.

18

The Every house was filling up with previously outlawed items. Since talking to his wife about the termites, Harlan began the long-buried process of softening his hard feelings. The place regained a certain woman's touches that had been boxed up and banned since the move out. He retrieved her final note from the attic and put it back up on the refrigerator with the heart-shaped magnet:

I forgive you.

Technically, they were still married. They called the separation a "trial," but that was five years ago. For the first time since the split he allowed himself to acknowledge her as his wife. He thought sweet thoughts, reread old love letters, built her in effigy from pillows, and squeezed her longingly—not murderously, as he had done in the past. He arranged the pillows under the covers so it looked like a sleeping body. He'd shut the lights, leave the bedroom, and come back later. He'd pretend to be quiet, tiptoeing so as not to wake her, then sliding under the covers, holding her into the night.

All the while, he kept reading the ledger, living vicariously through the dizzy saga of a boy who thought he'd found his girl. It was a strangely satisfying period. He spent quality time with his ink-and-paper son, and when his eyes went blurry, he crawled into bed with his foam-and-feather wife. He added verisimilitude by blowing up old pictures into free-standing, life-size companions placed strategically around the house: at the foot of his bed, by the stairs, in the kitchen. "Good morning," he'd say to a pregnant Hannah, photographed in 1973 in front of the Doral Hotel in Miami Beach. "Nice lid, pal," he'd say to Henry, photographed in 1977 beneath a giant sombrero on a family vacation to Mexico. "What happened to *you?*" he'd say to himself, photographed smiling, leaning out the window with a baseball bat, banging icicles off the gutter after the blizzard of '78.

For dinner he cooked the meals he used to mock, her old favorites, mostly vegetarian. That she'd since turned into a meat-eater with a yen for beef Wellington was not important — this was a re-creation of the past, prewar, and he was going for period authenticity. He let his sideburns grow and sat around in clothes he'd worn in the early seventies. He sprayed her favorite old perfume, Estee Lauder's Youth Dew, on her chair. He spoke out loud at the table about the allure of the Symbionese Liberation Army, the catchy-creepy treacle of the Carpenters, Evel Knievel's crash at Snake River, and, of course, ants.

One night, after preparing her favorite dessert — chocolate fondue with shortbread — he decided to make a list of things he'd always felt he should have apologized for.

1. When I rolled my eyes and made you feel stupid for never having heard of Galahad, the flawless son of

Lancelot and one of the three — with Percival and Bors — to achieve the Holy Grail. I read the Cliff's Notes in college.

2. When you came to bed naked and ready, and I said, "Sex with your wife is like getting an unwrapped present." I was just trying to be witty.
3. When I'd pretend to sleep as you cried. I know you always knew I was pretending. I have no excuse for this.

Hours later, he popped a Fiorinal and poured his last mug of gin for the night, reading and rereading a note she once taped to his chest as he slept.

It's amazing that someone who knows so much about the human body can know so little about people. I think it's time we laid all our stars out on the table.

19

"The jellyfish have eyes!"

Henry's father greeted his son with this revelatory piece of information as he walked through the door from his long weekend in New York. Dad was in his stinger suit, holding his trusty plankton net like a scepter. "They're registering gradations of light!" His fingers were orange from the brine shrimp nauplii he'd taken to raising and harvesting—far better than store-bought food, fresh shrimp made nutritious meals for the jellies.

"Fan*tastic*," said Henry.

"The Irukandji, he's responding."

"Perfect," said Henry. "I mean it, Dad. That's really perfect."

Fantastic? Perfect? This new tone was perhaps the only thing that could have jarred the old man out of the depths he'd inhabited since the tanks arrived. "What did you say?"

Henry unslung his backpack. "The Irukandji is important to you."

Henry's father dropped the plankton net. "What's the matter?"

"Nothing," said Henry. "Perfect."

"Stop saying that!"

"What? What's not perfect about it?"

"About what?"

"This—*any* of this. You in your suit with your orange hands and your net, discovering the secrets of the deep. And me—coming home to find things just as they were, only one hundred percent different."

"What's different?"

Henry started up the stairs. "Have you seen my hatchet?"

Jorden had been losing sleep for months. She'd stay up late thinking about Henry and keeping a watchdog's eye on her dad, listening for groans in the bathroom, creaks of the fridge, crinkles of wrappers. She routinely searched his belongings for danger signs: laxatives, diuretics, diet pills, ipecac. And she kept an eye on the rattraps; the critters had infested their attic (where he sometimes snuck to eat).

Henry walked over to her house, hatchet in pocket, and threw a stick at her window—over the shoulder, long and soaring. He hit the pane, but it stayed shut. He threw another. No lights went on. After a couple of minutes, he turned to leave. Jorden's dad pushed open the screen door and came out onto the farmer's porch. He was wearing a smock, dipping his index finger in a jar of aioli mayonnaise.

"Every, m'boy," he said, but the exclamation point was gone.

"Hiya," said Henry. "No bubbles tonight?"

"No bubbles," said Jorden's dad, sucking his finger. He looked saggy in his skin, off-color. There was blood on his smock.

"Is she napping?" Henry tried not to stare at the blood. "I threw a stick at her window . . . like you showed me."

"Disappointed?"

"In what?"

Jorden's dad put down the mayonnaise. He was clearly in the mood to talk. "I don't know, anything?"

"I'm only fifteen," said Henry lightly.

"It's relevant *especially* to a fifteen-year-old. That's when it starts." He produced an ice cream sandwich and pulled the whole thing out of the wrapper. In a bite, it was half gone. He seemed more energized as he swallowed. "Lemme explain something to you, son. And this'll save you a lot of time out there." He took another bite. "Nobody has ever improved on the ice cream sandwich."

"Okay," said Henry.

"No jimmies, no fluff, no oversized cones."

"Ice cream sandwich," said Henry. "No funny business."

Jorden's dad wiped his mouth on the back of his wrist. "You ever settle on a sport?"

"I didn't," said Henry. "I decided that I couldn't really commit. I couldn't *root.* I figure a person's got only so much rooting in them."

"And you're saving yours for something else."

Henry told him all about the pretty phantom. "I'm moving to New York."

"Does Jorden know?"

"Not yet," said Henry.

"So you're rooting for you."

Henry hadn't thought of it like that.

Jorden's dad got that old "gather 'round" look in his eye. It had been a while, but Henry still liked listening to him pontificate. "Know your audience," he'd say, and he did. With Henry he'd always whittle it down to a nugget. "Keep your expectations low," he said.

"Sorry?"

"That's your armor, your code. Your preemptive strike."

"For what?"

"For everything. This girl—*everything*. Beware of pretty phantoms. Don't put all your hearts in one basket." He sounded a lot like Henry's mother, only his phrasing was intentional. "Disappointment is a parasite; expectation its host. If you don't set it up, it can't knock you down. Just lower the bar. If it hits you in the shins—too high."

Henry pushed his lip up and out, nodding like his father. "Makes sense."

"What's the nugget then?"

Henry cracked his knuckles. "Marry an ice cream sandwich."

There followed a silence. Henry thought of the senior citizens and wondered if cynicism was inevitable.

Jorden approached the porch from the road. She was carrying a sleeping bag and a canteen. She seemed tired, her eyes blank and glassy.

"Hi, all," she said. "Hi, Henry."

"Hi," said Henry, touching the hatchet in his pocket. "What's the sleeping bag for?"

Jorden shrugged.

"What's in the canteen?" asked her dad.

"Apple juice." It was really chocolate malted milk—their favorite—but this time it was mixed with a little Bailey's Irish Cream. She didn't lie because of the alcohol: She didn't keep milk in the refrigerator anymore because her father would drink it all then throw it up. She squinted, pointing to the blood on his smock. "What's that?"

"Attic," said Jorden's dad, touching the smudge. "I strangled a rat."

Henry and Jorden walked the quarter mile to the bike rack. They didn't sit in their usual position. It would have been a bit awkward, considering the months of silence, for him to lie in her lap. He was taken aback when she stretched out and put her head on him. Instinctively, he twirled her hair.

"Think this rack will always be here?" he wondered. "Bikes aren't going anywhere, are they? Kids will always ride bikes. They'll always need bike racks and this one's as good as any. Can't really improve the old bike rack." He touched the metal bars and thought of all the knobby tires he'd worn down over the years.

"I had sex tonight," said Jorden.

Henry stopped twirling her hair.

"That's what the sleeping bag was for. We did it outside. *Al fresco,* they called it."

"They?"

"Mope Pope and Gimmel."

"Mope Pope? *And Gimmel?*"

"Did you know she's a chronic blusher? Really, it's a real condition." She was babbling, avoiding his eyes. "There's this procedure called an endoscopic thoracic sympathectomy where they insert small scopes through the armpit and basically just snip all the nerves in the face that make a person turn red—they can actually stop you from blushing. And Mope Pope, he has really tiny feet, he's very embarrassed about it, he kept his boots on the whole time—"

"Stop dancing," said Henry.

Jorden knew what that meant. "They invited me, told me to bring my sleeping bag. It was a scavenger hunt—"

"You had *sex* tonight?"

She shrugged. "We were a team. It was worth fifty points. A stolen bowling pin was ten, shaving your eyebrows, fifteen—"

"When?"

"About two hours ago. It's not at all like make-believe. But what is, right?"

This whole conversation felt like make-believe to Henry. He sat up and faced her. "You go from playing hide-and-go-seek and tag and juggling and wearing mismatched clothes and then all of a sudden you're wearing perfume and—"

"Why are you raising your voice?"

"Sorry," said Henry, checking to see if she'd pierced her ears. She hadn't.

"That's okay," said Jorden.

Henry didn't know why he was raising his voice. He felt more mature than he had five minutes ago, more conscious— of accountability, repercussions, stakes. He didn't just have sex, but his reaction was no less profound a passage. It felt foreign, almost parental. He was sad that she'd squandered something so big and precious, something she could never get back. And she didn't seem to care.

"We can still eat meals together, right?"

"Yeah," said Henry, distracted.

"Are you mad?"

"No," said Henry.

"Sad?" said Jorden.

"I'm not mad."

Jorden kneeled in front of him. "We could watch anything you want while we eat."

Henry pulled bunches of blades from the lawn. Jorden leaned in and tried to kiss him. He went with it, but only because he felt bad rejecting someone so blatantly. He would have kissed *any*one in that scenario. He'd thought of touching Jorden many times, but now all he could think about was Mope Pope's boots. Jorden kept kissing, her hands covering his ears. She was getting passionate, arching her back.

"Hey," said Henry, removing his lips, hoping to recontextualize the awkward moment. "Thanks for that hatchet. That was really cool."

Jorden unhooked her bra. "What hatchet?"

The night ended when Henry sheepishly told her about Benna. He stuttered when he mentioned his plans to "m-move on" to New York the following week.

"Move on?" she said. "From what?"

"Not from anything," he said, tapping his front tooth with his thumbnail.

Instead of probing she pulled back, hurt. "I think you should," she said, standing up. "You should go." She stared at him for a moment, forced a smile, and ran home to check the traps for roof rats.

That night she wrote Henry a letter titled "The One Who Got Away." It was all about how she really did want to be eating meals with him twenty years from now, and how, if he didn't rub his eyes, and quick, she would become that girl for him: *the one who got away.* When she finished, she read it over, then tore it up.

A week later she wrote again, avoiding her feelings.

Mope Pope is duller than peat moss. He's full of bunkum. Totally cracked. Gimmel said he's always staring in the mirror, and if you ever call him on it or ask him why, he'll make up something deep sounding, like "I just enjoy people-watching." Or "Just making sure I'm still here." She said he's obsessed with his legacy. Who's obsessed with their *legacy?* Anyway, she broke up with him after the scavenger hunt.

In Henry's absence the girls had become best friends. It was Gimmel who had left the hatchet by Henry's locker. She was sick of seeing them fight and hoped that maybe the four of them could double date.

All this was written in the letter, addressed to the Alcazar, where Henry had just checked in. The morning after the kiss at the bike rack he'd politely asked his father for permission to take the term off from school.

"Not a chance," said Dad. "You belong in class."

Henry tried appealing to his heart of hearts, still beating, he hoped, beneath all that Lycra. "You have your jellies," he reasoned. "I have Benna."

There was a flutter. Henry's father gave the nod. "You have the weekend to tame her. Friday night, Saturday, Saturday night, and Sunday afternoon. After that, home."

Henry was outraged. He was about to say something like "That's why Mom left you!" Instead he said, "She's not a fucking fish!"

"They're not *fish*. They're *Cnidarians!*"

"I'm moving," said Henry.

"You're not," said Dad.

Henry pounded up the stairs, two at a time, and started loading his duffel with fundamentals, including an envelope filled with money. Earlier that day he'd emptied his savings and pawned off the booty he'd plundered during his brief stint with Nika: two auto-reverse Walkmans, four rhinestone Swatches, a pair of Ray-Bans.

"You're *not*," said Dad, standing in the doorway. "Period, the end."

Henry kept packing, the wind gusting strong through his sails, the clapping crowds verging on pandemonium.

Henry's father couldn't possibly have known that his last three words to his son would prove so prophetic.

20

The Alcazar was a four-star hotel designed to look like a weather-beaten villa on the coast of someplace warm and rich with history. The pastel lobby was filled with rustic fruit bowls and columns, the cracked stucco walls painted to look as if they hadn't been touched up since the 1950s. There were only twelve rooms, each with its own decorative theme, all named after popular songs. "Home on the Range" had cedar saddle racks, barnwood dressers, and buckaroo beds with rope-style molding and horseshoe drawer pulls. "When You Wish Upon a Star" was for interstellar explorers, the domed ceiling specked with glowing celestial bodies, the minifridge stocked with Tang and vacuum-packed, freeze-dried astronaut snacks. "Misty Mountain Hop" catered to camping fans, complete with authentic antler chandeliers, handcrafted canoe bookshelves, and a skylight cut above a tent for two. Henry's room, appropriately, was "How Deep Is the Ocean?" There were kerosene cabin lamps, polished brass portholes for windows, and a waterbed mounted on four replicas of nineteenth-century clipper ship blocks. Henry fingered the scrimshaw on the sea chest, slipped the complimentary patch over his right eye, and unpacked his duffel. He hadn't told Benna he was coming.

Page 2103: color-coded pink

12/2/88

There are no uphill oceans, but this sure feels like one. We've entered uncharted waters. Hostile. Shark-infested. Far from land. My father sat really quiet on the sofa as I left, his arms crossed, his stinger suit zipped up all the way. In-de-*struct*-ible. His helmet hid his face, but I could tell he was thinking about the day Mom left. I don't think he'll swim after me. He's afraid of sinking so he just kind of floats. Like one of his jellies.

The concierge at the hotel looked at me funny when I pulled out the cash for the room. Like I was a bank robber or something. I don't much look like a bank robber, though. Maybe he thought I was part of an entourage, or a crew. Like I was a funnel for the cash, and the real guy, the top dog, was back at the hideout or something, getting more guns. I have no real interest in being part of a crew and robbing banks and stuff like that. I've always wondered, though: Why don't bank robbers go in at night? Banks close early, they'd have plenty of time. Why do they always go in during business hours, when there's people around? I mean, these guys seem to know what they're doing, a lot of them anyway — you'd think that one of them would have figured out a way to rob a bank at night. If they did, and I was invited, I'd probably go with them, just for the thrill. But only if I was invited.

Why did I show up here then? Unannounced and uninvited? Well, for one thing, I *was* invited. Sort of. It was late that first night, after the Ettinger reunion. We were up in Benna's room, the "Monster Mash" suite. It looked like a castle, with real stone walls, flickering candle bulbs, and a closet full of costumes and makeup. Above her bed was a vintage poster for *The Unknown*, a silent movie about a circus knife-thrower who cuts off his arms to win the love of a beautiful Gypsy who hates to be touched.

So we're up there, and after finishing our waffles and fruit shakes and champagne, we engaged in a series of highly competitive thumb wars. We were each in costumes from the closet: She was dressed as Death, with a black mask and sickle; I was dressed as her most recent victim, my clothes torn and bloody. I kept letting her win, trying to keep my left thumb smushed under hers for as long as possible. After the fourth game I asked what happened to her hand. "Boo-boo," she said. I wasn't sure if she meant an injury or a mistake and she didn't seem to want to elaborate. Then out of the blue she kissed me on the cheek and said I was "mercurial." I'm not sure what she meant exactly, but I've spent every day since trying to live up to her generous estimation. Anyway, I think that counts as an invite.

After unpacking, Henry attempted to spruce himself up. He took a shower, used lots of complimentary soap, shampoo, and conditioner. He moisturized his hands, thoroughly brushed his teeth and tongue, and arranged his hair as best he could. He put on his most comfortable clothes: linen pants, flip-flops, and a short-sleeved button-down shirt. It was early December; he was dressed to stay in.

Benna's room was on the top floor. He soft-shoed up the stairs, down the hall, and stood tall in front of her door. He chose to knock twice. Once, he thought, she might not hear; three times was coplike. Then he panicked. *I should have brought a present. Some flowers, maybe, or some candy.* He used to think flowers and candy made really corny presents, but Jorden once explained that corny can be good—girls actually like that stuff—and since they're the ones getting the gifts, that's all that matters.

Henry took off.

"New Yorkers must be the corniest people in the world," he later wrote in his ledger. "There's a flower stand on every corner."

He stopped at a stand on Christopher Street. "No roses," he told the flower man, a Korean hippie in overalls. He'd bent enough to buy the pretty things, but roses were out of the question.

"For a girl?" said the flower man.

"*The* girl," said Henry.

"Orchids are aphrodisiacs. Named after"—he whispered and pointed toward Henry's groin—"the penis."

At first this seemed like a great idea. But then he thought, *What if she knows it means penis? She'll think I'm trying to put one over on her.*

He wound up buying her a bushel of fresh-picked bananas from a fruit stand across the street. There were about forty of them, all bunched together on one stem. "From Monkey Point, Costa Rica," said the seller. "Organic." Henry thought the bananas looked exotic, as pretty as any flower, and hauled the bushel back to the Alcazar.

Again, he squared off against Benna's door, knocked twice, and waited. No answer. A housekeeper walked by holding pillows.

"Excuse me," said Henry. "Sorry, but would you by any chance happen to know the whereabouts of the young lady from the Monster Mash suite? Miss Benna?" It was clear from their night together that everyone knew Miss Benna. Indeed, it seemed, the housekeeper knew something but was unwilling to part with the information.

"Out," she said, protective, looking the bananas up and down. Henry wasn't sure if she was giving him a hint, or telling him to leave.

"Thank you," he said, taking a seat on the floor.

He waited. The housekeeper occasionally peeked out from around a corner to see if he was still there. After a while, he got hungry. He plucked a banana. A little after nine he put the bushel in his room and walked over to surprise Papi and Lulu. They were only a few blocks away.

Calvin wasn't around, so Henry buzzed the second floor. No answer. He could hear dance music coming from the roof. Feeling apelike after carrying the bushel, he decided to climb up the fire escape. It was very warm for December, almost sixty degrees. Henry pulled himself up to the ledge. Cast-iron gas lamps illuminated the roof garden. Papi was showing Lulu how to dance sexy in a club. They were drunk.

"This is the Wop, like this," said Papi. She dipped her shoulders, shimmied her head from side to side, stuck out her butt. "This is how we do it," said Papi. "Come on now, Mami! Wop with me!"

Lulu stayed seated, barefoot, her purple silk mules lined up side by side under the picnic table. "Oh sure, I'm just the one to Wop," she said sarcastically, sipping her drink. "Do the Cabbage Batch again. I like it when you do that one."

"*Patch*," said Papi, putting fist on top of fist, stirring an imaginary cauldron. "It's all in the hips," she said, humping

- 122 -

the air, slightly out of breath, loving the attention. "Hips and shoulders."

Henry looked on from the fire escape. He stayed for a while, just watching. It was such a nice moment, he didn't dare disturb it.

It was almost ten o'clock when Henry returned to the Alcazar. In the lobby there was fresh-bagged popcorn in an old-fashioned machine. He shuffled through, grabbed a bag without breaking stride, and went upstairs to retrieve the bananas.

Again he knocked on Benna's door. Twelve times in a row. On the thirteenth, she appeared, quickly closed the door behind her, and stepped into the hallway. "Henry?!" she said. She was wearing the same black mask and carrying the same sickle in her left hand. Henry handed her the bushel.

"For me?" she said, flirty. Her lips looked kissed.

"I could come back," said Henry, not really meaning it.

She gritted her teeth. "Could you?"

Henry sank.

The day after the reunion, he had written: "The great love stories always involve a chase, an obstacle, something to keep you glued. Not this one. This one's instantaneous. Presto!"

Presto, he thought, walking down the hallway to his room. *More like moron. Idiot.* He kicked open the door, pulled the patch over his eye. He stared condescendingly at his reflection. "How could I—I, Henry Every, *Captain* Henry Every—be so oblivious to the possibility of impending doom?"

He took a bottle of Caribbean spiced rum from the mini-bar, poured himself a healthy glass, then another. He pretended he was an alcoholic, that he'd been craving that first sip of the day. He closed his eyes, sniffed the liquor, went

"Aaaahhhh" as he swallowed. He'd read once that alcoholics don't get drunk, they just feel less bad. Well, Henry couldn't feel any worse. And pretty soon there was no more pretending: He was sloshed.

Hours later, there was a series of soft knocks on the door. He stumbled over and, with his uncovered eye, looked through the peephole. It was Death.

21

The annual American AntFest had a roving home, held in a different location each year. Last year it was in Madison, Wisconsin. The winner of the farm competition used the *Polyergus rufescens* species to successfully show a tribal slave raid. A band of marauding red Amazon ants stormed a rival nest, chewed up the queen, and kidnapped a colony of workers who were subsequently turned into servants. On the front of the exhibit was a sign: PROVERBS 6:6 — "GO TO THE ANT, THOU SLUGGARD; CONSIDER HER WAYS AND BE WISE." Spectators cheered the coup.

This year the festival was to be held in Lenox, Massachusetts, not far from the Every house. Harlan sent his wife a plane ticket. He was inspired by the rantings of his lovey-dovey son.

Page 2104: color-coded orange for "rising"

12/3/88

Benna, benchmark, benighted, beneficial, benediction, benevolence, benefactress . . . This girl was named correctly. This girl's good. I was drunk as hell, but the moment's crystal clear, polished, preserved. She makes me feel flowery. Corny. Like a poet. She's the marshmallow in a bag of charcoal. The branch in the rapids that saves me. She came to my room, dressed as Death, carrying a few extra pillows. "Wanna have breakfast tomorrow?" In the morning there was proof. The phone rang. "Hungry?" she said.

I was starving. I was starving and I was jealous of the phone receiver, so close to her mouth.

Even after Henry's death, Hannah continued writing weekly letters. She simply mailed them to herself, then filed them in a drawer. "Henry can read them from anywhere," she reasoned. She'd tell him about her day, what she ate for breakfast, the songs she'd been humming in the shower. She'd tell him things she wouldn't tell anyone else. But she'd never ask questions.

Ten days after the funeral she told him Dad had sent a ticket and she was coming home. The letter was standard length, about a page. When she finished, she reread it as if through his eyes. The words *coming home* sounded terrible. *What took so long?* She stared at them as if they were the only words on the page, then the only words in the world. Years of buried guilt and shame snaked their way through her body. She felt sick. She thought of his coffin, the cinnamon buns with extra icing. She nervously teethed on her knuckles, a habit, smelling the wet skin. She crumpled the letter and started over, drawing perfect pictures of Henry from memory. She rubbed her charcoaly fingers all over his face, then hers, then his, as if the blending would somehow foster contact. She wrote through pages and pages of peach-colored paper, stringing missing words together in the hopes of forming a coherent excuse for leaving home. For somehow causing his death. Not that she wanted to free herself from blame—she didn't. She wanted to pay, dearly. She focused on the regret, willed it into something tangible, holding it, kneading it, smashing it against the wall. She sobbed, scribbling, her face gray and blotchy—*weakness, coward, healing, guts*—and in the morning the letter wasn't even close to finished. It would never be finished.

Meanwhile, Harlan prepared the house for her arrival, stowing the life-size photos and the note from the refrigerator, redoing the rooms with long-stemmed roses and relics. He made up the guest room but also cleared a space for her clothes in their old closet.

22

Henry offered Benna a sip of his blueberry breakfast shake — "a house specialty," said the waiter at the Matinee. It was an old nickelodeon that had been converted into a twenty-four-hour diner. Benna vouched for the bacon. She took a pull from Henry's straw, then shook her head. "I like fresh blueberries better than blueberry shakes," she said. "But I like strawberry shakes better than fresh strawberries." She scooped a pile of soft-scrambled eggs. "Here." She nodded. "Good."

Henry took the fork in his mouth. It was the first time fowl had passed his lips since he was a little kid. He focused on the fork — *her* fork — as opposed to what was on it. He wasn't eating baby bird, he was eating Benna.

"More, please," he said. He had completely forgotten about her kissed lips the night before. As she scooped another forkful, Henry noticed a photograph of W.C. Fields above their table. "That's W.C. Fields," he said, taking another bite of Benna.

She picked up a crispy strip of thick-cut bacon. "Idol of yours?"

"He started out as this really terrific juggler. My friend Jorden's really into juggling, she told me all about—" Henry felt terrible, talking about juggling to a one-handed girl. He segued. "See, my dad's kind of a perfectionist. My friend thinks that's boring, she likes things rougher, she likes mistakes, so she once used W.C. to prove her point, that's all. She's always proving points."

"Sounds annoying."

"It isn't," said Henry, defensive.

Benna shrugged. "So W.C. . . . ."

"So he was this juggler," he began, hearing Jorden as he spoke. "And he never dropped a ball. And people liked him, they clapped for him. They clapped, but they didn't cheer. W.C. wanted cheers. Then one day he dropped a ball and everybody laughed. So he kept dropping them. He'd curse the balls and then himself and then give it another go. The more he cursed, the louder the laughs, and eventually he got his cheers."

"But not for what he set out to get them for."

"I guess he just wanted a reaction."

"That's what my parents say about me. That I always want attention, like a little kid."

"Don't we all?" said Henry.

"I guess. But who ever really pays attention? Nobody." She cracked her knuckles against the table. "See, that's what happens when nobody pays attention. You start having conversations with yourself. Asking yourself questions and answering them. Asking? Answering. Asking?"

"Answering," answered Henry.

Payalaya night—Lulu's favorite—came roughly every three weeks. The kitchen would fill up with strainers and skillets and the smells of fresh garlic, cayenne pepper, andouille sausage, and a hint of brown sugar. No chicken, of course. Papi was commander-in-chief, dressed in her red-checkered apron, waving her wooden spoon. Lulu, in a blue-checkered apron, stood a few inches behind her, watching closely as she'd mince and sprinkle. She never understood how Papi got her food to taste so good. And Papi had no intention of telling. She'd keep decoy ingredients on the counter just to throw Lulu off. The spices she did use, the magic ones, flashed and vanished like fireflies.

"F-Man called again," said Papi, fluffing the rice. "While you were at the beauty parlor." Her voice sounded different. It was softer, less ethnic, more refined. She'd switched her door-knocker earrings for tasteful studs and buffed the sparkles off her nails. Her painted sneakers had been replaced by purple silk mules.

"Who?" said Lulu, examining a diversionary jar of cumin.

"From school, the one you've been chasing." It was jarring; her gerunds now had g's. Not that Lulu noticed. She was noticing less and less these days.

"Efram. His name is *Efram*. And I am not—what did you say? *Chasing* him?"

The phone rang. "Yes?" said Papi, tasting the tomatoes, the phone in the crook of her neck. "Speak English, Calvin. *English*. All right then." She hung up. "Damn wetbacks."

"Calvin's not a wetback," said Lulu, touching a tomato. Papi knocked her knuckles with the spoon. Lulu shook her hand and backed off. "He's Puerto Rican."

Papi sliced the sausage into half-moon wedges. "What's the difference?"

"Are *you* a wetback?"

Papi held the knife up, threatening.

Lulu curtsied. "You'd miss me."

"I don't miss," said Papi.

"No," said Lulu. "You'd *miss* me."

There was a knock on the front door. "That's your grandson," said Papi, putting the knife down. "Or whatever he is."

Lulu walked out and opened the door, something she rarely did.

"Hi," said Henry, waving.

"Hi!" said Lulu, hooking his arm. "Are you hungry, dear? Papi's getting dinner ready."

"Smells like a real restaurant in here," said Henry.

"Do you take a drink?" She offered him a sip from her glass. "Papi makes it. Vodka and fresh pineapple, that's it. It's *won*derful."

"If it's wonderful," said Henry.

She escorted him into the kitchen. "You know Henry," she said to Papi.

Papi was deseeding a cucumber. "Like an x-ray," she said.

23

Harlan sat waiting for his wife at the airport. He was early, dressed in a casual suit, no tie. He felt that conveyed the proper mix of excitement and informality. As he watched women lug bags from the carousel he thought of all his mistakes: how he'd disengage, how he fake-slept as she cried.

When he saw Hannah stepping off the escalator, he didn't leap to his feet. All he could see was the space between them and all the time that they'd been apart. He felt anxious, like this was the last real test, and if he failed, that's it, that's the end. He stayed seated and wished he were Galahad.

Hannah came over and dropped her bag on his feet. She patted his head. "Your hair's short."

"I just got a haircut." Harlan stood up, nervous, and grabbed her bag. She was a good foot shorter than him. "Remember my sideburns?"

"Chopsticks, you called them." She paused. "Chopsticks?"

"Pork chops," he said.

This type of error used to annoy him. He'd get mad, really mad, and she'd say, "That's what you should love *best* about me," and he'd ask "Why?" Now he knew why.

"It's good to see you," he said.

"Me too," she said, affectionately scratching his shoulder. She looked up at him. "We should hug hello. I could squeeze you, or you could squeeze me, or we could squeeze each other—"

Harlan dropped the bag and gave her a hug worthy of a gum commercial. As he lifted her, she bent her legs at the knees. Their cheeks pressed together. When he put her down he flexed the biceps in his right arm. He hadn't flexed in some time. It was something he used to do a lot with her; they'd be lying in bed or out getting ice cream, and he'd ask her to feel his muscle. "Feel," he'd say. Sometimes she'd bite it. He liked it best when she'd bite.

"I've been thinking about the ant farm competition," he said, as they pulled out of the airport. "I was thinking it might be awesome to have an underwater terrarium."

"Awesome?" The word sounded funny out of his mouth. And he'd never paid much attention to her ants.

"Yeah," he said. "As I'm sure you're aware, some ants can live for up to two weeks underwater. So I was thinking we could show how."

"We?"

He kept his eyes on the road.

"We?" she said again.

"Yeah," he said, gripping the wheel.

She thought about putting her hand on top of his. She pictured their fingers intertwined as they steered off the turnpike, past Henry's high school, past the pet store, past the movie theater, past the market, past Jorden's house, and into her old spot in their heated two-car garage.

24

Before Benna, Henry had kissed just two girls in his life (not including Jorden). It had always felt strained. He was too aware of the process. Too focused on their tonsils and their taste buds. He got to second base once on the golf course, up the cut-off sweatshirt of an eighth grader who kept her bra on, so it wasn't *really* second, but he considered it so. Benna was a whole other galaxy, much warmer, with her own set of winds and currents. And she knew what she was doing.

On their twenty-second night together, she described her home life as "occasional." She said she didn't know her parents very well. "My parents aren't parents," she said. "They're people who had kids." She said she didn't mind, that it gave her the freedom "to branch out." But Henry could tell she missed having her roots around.

"Do you ever stare at your feet and feel like they're so far away?" said Benna. "Like they're not really *yours?*" She and Henry were lying on the bed in her room, wearing costumes from the closet. Henry was dressed as a changeling in a green suit and hat. Benna was wearing a black frock, eating gummy bears.

"I do," said Henry. "I really do think that sometimes. Only it's not just my feet, it's everything. Like my whole body's a body suit."

"For me it's just my feet," said Benna. "I stare at them and feel like even if I tried to wiggle them, I couldn't. Like all of a sudden they're gonna stop cooperating." She put a red gummy bear between her front teeth. She had a method: slowly bite their heads off.

"Have you ever broken a bone?"

"No, but I always wanted to," said Benna. "I wanted people to sign my cast." She bit the head off a clear bear.

"Is it true that some people — people without arms or legs — is it true that they can sometimes feel, like, a *phantom limb* or something? Is that what it's called?" He'd heard the term from Jorden. "Like, they can feel what's missing? Like what's missing is there?"

"Some people can," said Benna. "For me, though, what's missing is missing." She was staring at her toes. Henry noticed, made his way down her body, and kissed her big left toe. "Is this your foot?" he said.

She smiled, clicking her heels. He kept kissing, across her ankles, up her shin, over her knee. She touched his head, pulled off the green hat. "Come here, changeling."

Henry tugged at her frock. They ground their heads together. Her body felt snug, cozy. She made small noises as he moved on top of her.

"How are your feet?" he said, sloping off and lying next to her, his palm flat against her stomach.

"Perfect," she said, her left arm flung above her head, her right one flush against her side. "All mine."

"And the rest of your body?"

She smiled. "Very cooperative."

She rolled on top of him: chest to chest, pelvis to pelvis, her legs together between his. Henry held her left hand. With his right, he eagerly made his way toward her smooth, round wrist. She didn't pull away. It felt like the small end of a baseball bat, and for Henry it was far more exhilarating than getting to any of the proverbial bases. He pressed his wrist against hers and pretended to hold her right hand, as if what was missing was there.

A thump shook the door.

"Fuck!" said Benna, jumping.

Thump, thump.

"What the—"

"Ssshh!" she whispered, pushing him off the bed. "Go! Get up! Go to the bathroom!" She wrapped herself in a towel. "Get in the tub! Lie down in the tub, pull the curtain. *Turn the water on.*"

Henry did as he was told.

"Hello?" said Benna to the door.

"Hello," said the voice, a man.

"I'm in the shower," she said.

"So?"

"I'm in the *shower.*"

A key turned the lock.

Page 2195: color-coded yellow for "forward march"

12/31/88

Last night I dreamt of Nika. The new Nika, the false Nika. We were back in her basement, making tap shoes out of old sneakers and seashells. The turtle-man supplied the shells from his brown paper bag. Teddy was there, and he seemed happy. Eddie was spitting spitballs at people. My father was wearing his stinger suit, the Irukandji on his shoulder like a parrot. Mr. Van Putt was there in his warm-up suit, and Jorden, and Jorden's mom, who I've never met. There aren't many pictures of her around the house. I wonder if the woman in my dreams actually looks like her. Anyway, it was good to see them all, especially Nika. Even though we had nothing to do with the poisoning, I've always felt a little guilty. So it was nice that she kept thanking me for the transformation. "Thanks for redoing me," she said and handed me a friendship pin.

Efram's been trying to pin Lulu, but she seems pretty set on staying faithful to her husband. There's pictures of him all over the house. I say "her husband" instead of "my grandfather" because I never really knew him and it feels weird appropriating him. At dinner the other night she told me I could sit anywhere but at the head, which I thought was a little bossy for a grandma. But Papi later told me that's where he used to sit, so she likes to sit there as well. Made sense, and I felt bad for thinking she was bossy. She also uses the same plate and silverware for every meal — his plate and silverware. At first this made me really sad, but then I thought it was just about the nicest thing in the world. If Benna died I'd do the same thing.

The other night we sat around her room and made up Indian names for each other. Benna was Chief Littlewrist. I was Chief Monkeyface. This was before she left me in the tub for twenty minutes while she talked to her father in the hallway. She came back rattled and said he knew the whole time I was in there, and that I was lucky he didn't mangle me, and that my room was locked and I'd likely never see any of my stuff again. She said I couldn't stay there, that she was really sorry, but that she was prepared to flee with me, at least for a little while.

On New Year's Eve, Henry and Benna showed up at the corner of Fifth Avenue and Ninth Street with very few fundamentals. It was about eight-thirty. Henry was still dressed as a changeling.

"Mr. Henry?" said Calvin, confused by the costume.

"*Feliz navidad!*" said Henry.

"Happy New Year!" said Calvin, picking up the phone to announce their presence.

The door was open at the top of the stairs. They took off their shoes before entering. Henry heard water running in the bathroom. He walked over to the door, peeked in, and jumped. It looked as if Papi had scalped her boss. She was washing Lulu's wig in the sink. For Henry, this was almost as troubling—he didn't know she wore one.

"Hi, Papi," said Henry. "This is Benna."

"Hi, Benna," said Papi, turning around. "Benna?"

"My real name's Beatrice."

The television was off in the living room. Lulu hated watching the ball drop in Times Square. She hated anything to do with the passing of time. She was sitting in her high-backed red chair, sipping a White Russian, singing every word to Holla Fifer's "Big Bad Baby." She swung her drink to the rhythm, eyes closed, tapping her foot. She was wearing a glittery Betty Boop brooch. Her hair looked like it always did. Women with wigs, Henry learned in that instant, have more than one.

Lulu opened her eyes when Henry and Benna walked in.

She stayed seated and greeted them with her trademark wave; instead of a tick-tock motion she bent her wrist up and down, like the top of a crocodile mouth. It was almost like she was telling you to bow or get down. Benna misinterpreted the gesture and sat on the floor. Henry sat down next to her.

"Beatrice?" he whispered.

"My real name's Beatrice," said Benna.

Henry seemed very disturbed by this. "What do you mean your *real* name? What happened to it?"

Lulu interrupted with a call for drinks. "Spirits!" By the volume it was clear she was talking to Papi, who promptly entered holding the wig in a plastic bag. "'Round the room," said Lulu, meaning spirits for all. She rose from the chair, extra friendly from the booze. "Come on, I'll show you kids how to dance." Benna stood up, her dancing socks pulled high.

"Fox Trot," said Lulu. "Watch now." She took slow steps, then quick steps, moving in a square. "Slow-slow, quick-quick," she instructed, scooting around the room. "We used to clear the floor with this one."

Henry and Benna worked the steps into a sloppy jig, adding some twirls and dips. Papi returned and passed out the drinks. "Now this is dancing!" said Lulu, taking Papi's hand. "Not that Cabbage Batch business. Come on!"

Papi went with it, snapping her fingers to the $4/4$ beat. The song played over and over and pretty soon everyone was singing along, spilling their drinks on the Oriental rug. Henry sang, hopping: "Oh, the big bad baby with the brown eyes." Then Benna, spinning: "The big bad baby with the brown eyes." Then Papi, on tiptoes: "The big bad baby with the brown eyes." Lulu closed it out, glorious: "Big-*boy*, Big-*boy*, Big-*boy*."

They all collapsed on the rug.

"Jeepers crow," said Lulu, wheezing, checking her pulse.

"What's the matter?" said Papi, alarmed. "What is it?"

"Nothing."

"Every little noise I get nervous," Papi told Henry and Benna.

"What noise?" said Lulu. "What *noise* do I make? I don't make any noise."

"Keep quiet, Lulu," said Papi. "Just relax."

Lulu rolled her eyes. "That's gonna be the title of your biography—'Keep Quiet, Lulu.'"

The phone rang. Papi jumped to get it.

"She's always running for the phone, that one."

"Was that your favorite dance?" asked Benna.

"We used to dance to that song all the time," said Lulu. "My husband and me. He was a very elegant dancer." She looked right through the walls and into the past. "The Peabody, the Quickstep, the Roseland—"

"Always dancing," said Benna rhapsodically.

"It wasn't *always* dancing," said Lulu. "This was before he went into the service."

"You were a soldier's girl?"

"Oh sure, I was with him down in Hattiesburg, before they shipped him out. *Praise the Lord and pass the ammunition.* It was horrible. I remember a sign, it said 'No Dogs. No Jews.' A real pit. There were thousands of girls down there with their husbands. They lived there. They lived in cellars, in stores, they joined together and rented apartments. I stayed in a hotel. He was only a private but I lived like a general's wife."

"The Great War," said Benna, as if she'd lived through it.

"The *Good* War," corrected Lulu. "The Great War was the war to end *all* wars—which of course it wasn't. My husband, he got shot in the shin. He was awarded a Purple Heart. I used to wear it on a chain."

Henry sat back and observed. He loved hearing about his ancestors. And he loved that Benna was interested in listening to the aches of a stranger.

"What else did he love to do?" she asked.

"What did he love?" Lulu seemed happy to go back. "Well, he loved a good piece of mackerel. With butter and onions. Lots of onions. And corn. Native corn. We'd drive up to the farms and pick our own. He loved to drive. He loved to drive a car. He'd drive all the way to Paris if he could."

"Did you like to drive?"

She chuckled. "Not when he was in the car."

"Did you always know you'd end up with him?"

Lulu smirked. "When I was sixteen years old, I got a convertible. It was an aqua color with a big backseat, and my father put my initials on the side of the door, by the handle, in gold script. For my first ride, I went out looking for him—I wanted to show off a little. He wasn't my husband at the time, of course, but I used to run after him a little bit. He used to hang around—there was a place where all the boys used to hang around. So I put on my hat, and I drove by. And sure enough, there he was. And I asked him, 'Would you like to go for a ride with me?' And he said, 'No. I'm busy.' Just like that. 'I'm busy.' *Well.* I came home and I was hysterical. And my mother said to me, 'Why are you crying? What's the matter with you? If he didn't want to go with you, what do you care? You think he's such a *bargain?*' And I said, 'Well, Mother, he's a bargain to me.'"

"How did he propose?" said Benna, leaning in. It was clear that Lulu had not noticed her missing hand. As opposed to Papi, who, like most people, snuck peeks and said nothing.

"I went up to his house one night, and we were having some tea. I went to take a sip, but there was a box in my cup. And I said, 'What is that? Is that for me?' And I opened it up and it was a ring."

Benna smiled.

"Not anything that I would pick out, be*lieve* me, but anyway—"

This caught Henry's attention. "You didn't like the ring?"

"I didn't like it, I didn't want to wear it," said Lulu. "But I did. I wore it. I wore it all the time. Then I lost it. It's funny how I lost that ring. Either I lost it or somebody took it. And I was glad."

"What was wrong with it?" said Henry.

"Nothing," said Lulu. "It wasn't me, that's all. It just wasn't me."

At first Henry found the statement really obnoxious. But then he came to envy its clarity. As he sat wondering what type of ring was him, Papi came back smiling from her phone call. Her hair looked different.

"Who was that?" said Lulu, snapping back to the present.

"F-Man."

"Again?"

"I told him we were dancing."

Lulu squinted. "Why are you wearing my wig?"

Just before eleven o'clock, Papi put Lulu to bed and cleaned up. She practiced the Fox Trot as she wiped down the stove and covered the leftovers in cellophane. She was wearing the blue-checkered apron, Lulu's apron, moving slow-slow, quick-quick across the floor. Meanwhile, Henry and Benna were walking hand in hand outside on their way to a party for the Pilgrims — a group of people Benna said Henry would relate to. She said she went to gatherings every once in a while, and that tonight's speaker — a man named Andy — was particularly relevant.

"What's your greatest talent?" asked Henry, heading north on Fifth Avenue. "Besides kissing."

"People believe me."

"They trust you?"

"They say I have a frank face."

Henry stared at her profile. "I know that's a compliment but I wouldn't describe your face as frank."

"No?"

"No. It's too pretty. *Frank?*"

"Hey, that's how we met! Because of a frank!"

"The *lack* of a frank."

"What about you?" said Benna. "What's your greatest talent?"

"I used to be one hell of a pirate. Now I'm a pretty good spy."

"For real?"

"My friend taught me. The one who juggles."

"Who do you spy on?"

"Strangers."

Benna's face lit up. "Could you show me? I mean, could we do it? Together?"

"We *could*."

"Don't say *could* like that. My stepmom used to do that. I'd ask for something, for some candy or to go to the bathroom, like, 'Could I please go to the bathroom?' and she'd say, 'You *could*.' Or 'I don't know, *could* you?'"

"Sorry," said Henry. "My mom was very into manners, too."

"This is a stepmom, though. It's different."

"Who would you want to spy on?"

"Strangers," said Benna. "Sort of. My dad, he takes this camping trip every year with my stepbrother, to the middle of the woods. I've always wanted to go but my dad says it's only for boys. He always wanted a boy—I didn't get a dress until I was eight. I want to see what I've been missing."

"The middle of the woods?"

"Don't worry, I know what I'm doing. That's my other talent—I'd make a real good boy. I've paid attention my whole life, even took a bunch of courses. Survival stuff—in the actual woods. I thought that would make me eligible for the camping trip but . . ."

Henry tested her. "What's the best way to send a smoke signal? Should we need to."

"Evergreen boughs make the blackest smoke. Three fires is ideal—the most universally recognized stress signals come in threes. Even Morse code for SOS"—she tapped his shoulder —"*tap, tap, tap.*"

"And should we be lost and starving and need to hunt our own food? Then what?"

"I'm pretty good at grabbing grouse, frogs, owls, turtles, and—*mmmm*—rainbow trout."

"I don't really eat birds," said Henry.

"Okay, well, worst-case scenario, I can make a net, a killing pit, a figure-four deadfall—all from available material. Should catch us some fish or meat. And then there's local greens, acorns, berries, birch syrup, certain mushrooms. And insects are very nutritious, lots of fat, which is most important."

"Insects?"

"That's *worst* worst-case scenario. As for keeping our bearings, I can locate Polaris with my eyes closed, and if you lose your shoes I can carve moccasins from rawhide."

"Okay then, Crockett," said Henry, thoroughly confused but more than convinced. "Could I have a kiss now, sir?"

She smiled. "You *could*, and you *may*."

They walked west and stopped in front of a warehouse in the meatpacking district. It was 11:45. "What if you're lost, really lost?" said Henry. "Is it better to stay put or to wander?"

"Stay put," she said.

"I disagree," said Henry.

She pointed to an unmarked entrance. "We're here. Come on."

Henry followed Benna up a staircase dimly lit with bare bulbs and into a cavernous room on the third floor. There was no password; anybody could have walked in. About seventy people sat in metal folding chairs to hear Andy, the featured speaker of the night. Henry and Benna were late, so they just leaned against the back wall.

"My father always said that I took things for granted," Andy told the crowd. He was in a wheelchair; both of his legs disappeared at the knee. "He said I didn't take care of my things. That I didn't appreciate them. That I was careless. My father was a man who took *very* good care of his things. He was a maintenance nut, obsessed with safety and caution and cleanliness. He always took the stairs instead of the elevator. He wiped off the silverware in a restaurant. He never left home without a shave. And he never once told anyone how he truly felt. 'A person should respect boundaries,' he'd say. This was even before I had my legs cut off."

Henry got the chills. He thought of the conversation in bed at the Alcazar, before the thump shook the door.

"People always seemed a lost cause to my father," continued Andy. "It was the appreciation of *objects* he valued most. He never said to me 'Life is fragile, be careful not to break it.' Or 'Truth is precious, be careful not to get it dirty.' But when it came to my new bicycle, or the blender in the kitchen, or the way I tossed my clothes around? 'No respect,' he'd say. 'Taking things for granted.'

"I haven't spoken to him since the surgery. Rather, he hasn't spoken to me. No, I guess I didn't appreciate the body I was given. I always felt like I was conspicuous, like I was wearing a very obvious mask. Living somebody else's life. Cutting my toenails was the worst. Like I was cutting somebody *else's* toenails. See, when I thought of myself, in my mind, I was different.

"Then, about two years ago, I started pretending. Seeing what it would be like. I'd bind my shins to the back of my thighs and roll around in an old wheelchair. When people looked at me in the chair I felt normal. For the first time in my life, I felt comfortable, as if I *was* who I *was*. But the truth is, I wasn't. It was as much a disguise as any. So I looked into doing it for real. I found out about black market doctors in Mexico. I read up on anesthesia. I spoke to a guy in Scotland who performed the operation himself with a log splitter. Another guy buried his arms in dry ice and waited for the gangrene to get so bad that a doctor *had* to operate. But then I got very lucky. I was referred to a wonderful surgeon who helped turn me into me."

The crowd stood and cheered. It was one minute to the new year, and when P.M. turned to A.M. the clapping mushroomed into one of the greatest ovations Henry had ever heard. He wasn't simply listening to an anonymous roar—he knew what it was for and he felt part of it.

Andy bowed as best he could and wheeled down the ramp. His fellow Pilgrims shook his hand as they gathered around a table for refreshments: low-budget Oreo knockoffs and plastic cups filled with alcoholic bug juice. Clusters formed in corners, people checked each other out. It felt like a dance at a church—there was real kinship, community—but it was as if all the members had been blackballed, which made the bond even tighter.

Benna disappeared; Henry mingled. He met a Korean woman who, unhappy with her "lizard eyes," had saved up for a blepharoplasty, a cosmetic surgery that creates an upper eyelid. A white kid named Will, inspired by the book *Black Like Me*, shaved his head, injected collagen into his lips, and, in addition to marathon tanning sessions and skin dye, had started taking Oxsorlen, a pill he thought would "brown" him.

Page 2200: color-coded green for "do-over"

1/1/89

Arteries take fresh blood from the heart to the organs; veins bring the used blood back to the heart. When you stick a beating artery with a needle, the pressure is so high that bright red blood spurts out. When you stick a vein, the blood is more crimson and it just kind of dribbles. These are some of the things I learned from the Pilgrims. People here know a lot about surgery: everyone's been modified somehow—or *enhanced* — as many of them like to say. The main speaker at last week's session had a "cricothyroid approximation," a surgery that stretches your vocal cords. "My voice wasn't my voice," he told the group. "It was like a stranger was speaking through me. So I fixed it."

Some of the Pilgrims are into extreme body modification, like scarring and branding, and a few of the regulars have had sex-reassignment surgery. I talked loudly to a deaf female bodybuilder with a cochlear implant. A trepanation advocate who, after having a hole drilled through the front of his skull, claimed he was "enlightened." One guy called Split Jimmy has a forked tongue and little horns slipped under the skin on his forehead. "It's all the same shit," he said. "Some people wear makeup, get Mohawks, tattoos, piercings. Some suck their fat, some break the bones in their face. And some people cut off their hands and slip horns in their head. It's all the same shit."

Andy, a double amputee, is one of the more revered regulars. He's what some doctors call an "apotemnophile." There's a bunch of them here: people missing fingers, hands, but Andy really took it to another level. He paid a surgeon ten thousand dollars to sever both his legs below the knee. We shook hands and I was taken aback by the strength of his grip. We started talking and I told him how I'd always felt out of place, like my insides didn't match my outsides. I told him about the browsing, the cages filled with animals. He was very easy to talk to down there in his chair. I told him that my father's been trying to tame these deadly jellyfish, and that he walks around in a stinger suit, and that jellyfish have no brains. I asked him a million questions about his surgery, how they did it, how he liked it, and he told me if I wanted, he

would give me the number of his guy, Dr. Adam Kiewicz—
as long as I promised not to become a double amputee.
I promised and he gave me the number. I looked around for
Benna to thank her for bringing me, but she was gone. I
looked everywhere. Will said he saw her leave with Split
Jimmy.

Henry went back to Lulu's by himself and wrote all night
in his ledger. He was angry at Benna for leaving him alone on
New Year's Eve, but he was excited by what he'd seen. He sat
in a desk chair with wheels. He thought about the turtle-man
at the fountain and wondered what life would be like in a
wheelchair.

Around six o'clock in the morning he got up to go to the
bathroom. He heard Lulu in the kitchen on the phone: "Oh,
come on, F-Man—*Phyllis?* She's so cheap she wouldn't buy
the right time."

Henry listened to her talk as he peed.

"That *alter kocker?* Her taste is in her *mouth.*"

Henry put water on his fingertips and rubbed the sleepy
seeds from his eyes. That's what his mom used to call the crust
that formed as he slept. A bigger kid once teased him, said
they were eye boogers. "No," said Mom. "That boy is wrong.
Those are sleepy seeds. If you plant them, and water them,
and care for them, your dreams will grow."

"Really?" said Henry, seven years old.

"You could have a whole garden," she'd say. "Just be careful of the weeds."

"Weeds?"

"Nightmares," said Mom.

Henry dried his hands and wondered if Benna was a weed.

He pictured her kissing Split Jimmy with his forked tongue. He pictured Mope Pope's boots. He shut the light in the bathroom, walked into the kitchen, and almost had a heart attack.

"I have a girl who takes care of me—comes from a *wonderful* family," said Lulu into the phone.

Only it wasn't Lulu. It was Papi. She was wearing Lulu's wig.

25

"I still do the same things," said Hannah. She and Harlan were enjoying a nice beef Wellington in their old seats in their old kitchen. A bouquet of roses sat in the center of the table. "I still set the plates for dinner, but instead of two plates I set one. I go to the grocery, but instead of purchasing six tomatoes, I get three."

"Purchasing," said Harlan. "I love that you say that."

"Oh?" she said.

"I love it when you say stuff like that."

"Don't embarrass me."

"You wanna see something? I was looking through some old boxes and I found something I think you'd wanna see."

"What is it?" She really loved surprises. He could wrap a piece of cake in tinfoil — she'd light up as she tore into it.

Harlan got up from the table and pulled her chair out. They walked into the den. He dimmed the lights. "Close your eyes," he said.

She was excited, but there was something on her mind. "Okay, but before you wow me —"

"Who said anything about wowing?"

She patted the sofa. "Come, sit next to me."

Harlan sat down next his wife. "What is it?"

"How's the reading going?"

"Best book I've ever read. One of the only, but still. Henry's my new hero."

She knew he was reading in sequence now. "There's a part coming up—"

"Don't tell me! I want to get there myself."

Hannah leaned forward as if being pushed by a ghost.

"He's just moved in with my mother," said Harlan. "I can see why you like her. Once removed, she seems pretty okay. And Benna. Steamy. A little weird, the whole hand thing, but—"

"Do you regret falling off with your mother?"

"I wish she'd been different with me."

"Henry always regretted falling off with you."

Harlan seemed pleased by this.

Hannah closed her eyes and jumped. "You're not his father, Harlan."

The sentence stung. He took a breath before answering. "Look, I know I wasn't always—" He stopped short; she hated when he started sentences with *look*. It didn't even occur to him that she was telling the truth.

She tried again. "Harlan, please. You're not—"

"*You* weren't—"

"You're not his—"

"YOU THINK YOU WERE THE BEST—"

"No," she said, backing off.

They shared a guilty silence. "It's not too late," he said softly.

"No," she said.

"I'm making progress. Achieving. On a grand scale."

"I know you are."

"We're getting closer," he said.

She looked at the ceiling. Her husband hugged her and she hugged him back. *You're not his father,* she said again, this time to herself. *And I wasn't a mother.* She cleared her throat, leaned back into the sofa. "What was it you wanted to show me?"

Harlan walked over to the stereo and pushed play. It was the *Great Ovations* cassette that Henry used to carry around in his backpack. She hadn't heard it in years. The dub sounded more ominous than the real thing. Hannah sat pink-eyed on the sofa, the ghost lying quietly in her lap, the room filling up with applause.

The Every master bedroom always stayed dark for as long as the shades were drawn. Hannah used to wake up early and tiptoe out of the room. If she saw someone sleeping, no matter what time of day, she'd be extra quiet so as not to wake them. On this particular morning she crept downstairs and eased back into her old kitchen. She crowded the counter with ingredients for fresh tea, Swedish pancakes, and bacon. The previous night the couple had fallen asleep next to each other. Husband hugged wife from behind, happy to replace foam and feather with flesh and blood. Before bed, he read to her from the ledger.

Page 2210: color-coded yellow

1/2/89

Benna showed up at Lulu's at about 11:30, New Year's Day. I was furious, but so was she. It's hard to be furious at someone when they're furious at you. She said she left with Split Jimmy "for one second" to smoke a joint and when she came back I was gone. She waited and waited and waited, then left. She didn't want to call or come by because it was late and she didn't want to wake anyone up.

"Sorry," she said.

"Sorry," I said.

We made up, and then I asked her if she cut off her hand. She said no, that she was simply born without it, a fluke, but that she really likes hanging out with the Pilgrims. Kids were mean to her growing up — they called her "one-handed bandit" — and the Pilgrims were especially cool. It wasn't a victim's club, she said, these people *chose* to be like that, and that was comforting. They actually *wanted* to be like her. There was no pity, no sympathy. It made her feel better. I felt like chopping my hand off so she'd feel even less alone. I'd keep my right one so together we'd be whole-handed. I even asked her for the names of the kids who used to make fun of her. I told her we could go find them and egg their houses or something. But we just ended up calling information for their numbers and making a bunch of chicken calls. It made her feel better so I felt better, too.

Then she told me about what happened to her name. She changed it because her great aunt Beatrice was a racist. And not just a conversational racist, she actually did racist things. Benna says she protested the Little Rock Nine and helped out with at least one church bombing. I know a little bit about that stuff because Jorden's from Georgia, and that's a pretty backward place, racially speaking. They still have segregated proms and two homecoming queens — a black one and a white one. Jorden says it's a nice place, a traditional town where fathers and sons spend Saturdays dressed in camouflage, eating boiled peanuts and hunting deer. I always liked the idea of fathers and sons dressed in camouflage.

So anyway, that's why Benna changed her name, because Beatrice was a racist. I'm against name changes because they're usually done for really vain reasons, but this one sits fine with me. Benna's not vain. When you're born with one hand it's hard to be vain.

In Jorden's latest letter she said the roof rats were gone and that her father had started training for the Boston Marathon and putting up more pictures of her mother. Gimmel was getting back together with Mope Pope. She also said that my "love" for Benna was Ptolemaic. That I revolve around her. That her missing hand is the Earth, and I'm just a heavenly body.

The bacon was perfectly cooked, drizzled with maple syrup. Hannah wrapped the strips in pancakes then dusted them with powdered sugar. There were three to a portion—she called it Three Little Pigs. This was one of Henry's favorite breakfasts. His other favorite was her Humpty Dumpty, which was just a piece of white bread fried in butter with an egg in the cut-out center. Other mothers called it a Bullseye, or Rocky Mountain Toast, or Hole in the Bread, but for Henry it was always Humpty Dumpty.

"Did I snore?" asked Harlan. He was sitting at the table, waiting to be served, reading the ledger as if it were the morning paper.

"I wouldn't know," said his wife.

"You used to say I sounded like a disposal."

"I used to fall asleep second," she said, pouring orange juice for two. "Last night I fell asleep first."

"Henry never went to bed before three in the morning. He was an insomniac."

All she heard was the past tense. She thought about his coffin and her hands started shaking. The juice spilled.

Harlan read aloud from the ledger. "Listen to this, he wrote 'Kids who get scared and lie awake at night have greater imaginations than kids who sleep fine. How could kids *not* be scared of the unknown? They don't know anything!'"

Hannah steadied her hands, wiped up the orange juice, and brought the food into the breakfast room. It was awful for her to look at Henry's old spot at the table. He used to eat his Three Little Pigs in about forty-five seconds, and she'd say, "Slow down, no one's running after you." Harlan loved her cooking, too, and she felt better now watching him eat. When they finished, he began doing the dishes.

"You don't have to do that," she said.

"I don't mind," he said.

"Yes, you do."

"I don't."

"You *did*."

"Really," he said, scrubbing. "I want to."

"I wish you wouldn't." She took the sponge out of his hands. "Would you like it if I started washing the car? Or blowing the snow? Or banging icicles off the gutter? Just to please you?"

Harlan backed off. "Okay," he said. "Okay, wash the dishes."

"You wash the cars, I'll wash the dishes."

Harlan took the dishtowel from under the sink. "I'm drying."

26

Papi placed a fresh jar of spirit-melting water under her bed. It was just after dawn, but you could already tell it was going to be a sunny day. Henry sat tapping his front tooth in her black wicker chair. Papi paced, ashamed, walking barefoot over the witch pegs in her floor.

"There's an old story," she said, her hair slicked back. Her voice was now totally different. Shakier, more ladylike. More like Lulu's. "About a man who goes hunting in the woods and gets attacked by a wolf. The wolf goes for his neck, but the hunter pulls his knife and hacks off the wolf's paw. On his way home he stops by a friend's house to tell him what happened. But when he goes to show him the paw, it's no longer a paw. It's a woman's hand."

Henry stared at the black rag doll on the dresser. He felt very uncomfortable looking at someone in such a vulnerable state. He wished he'd never got up to go to the bathroom.

Papi continued, pacing. "The hunter stares at the hand. There's a ring on the finger, a wedding ring. He looks closer and screams. It's his wife's."

Henry was tapping at lightning speed.

"So the hunter goes looking for her. She's not in the

house. She's not in the yard. He finally finds her at the edge of the forest. He goes to hug her, but she keeps one hand in her pocket. The hunter pulls at her arm and is horrified to find that her hand is missing."

Henry, of course, was picturing Benna's wrist. He grimaced, making brief eye contact with Papi, then landing on a stack of books next to her bed: one on lycanthropy, one on shape shifting, one on etiquette. He stopped tapping his tooth. "You've changed," he said, looking directly at her. "Your voice, everything."

"That's what I'm trying to explain."

"You want to chop off my paw?"

"Don't be a dummy," she said. "You're the hunter."

Henry was confused but happy to be the hunter. "Why were you pretending to be Lulu?"

Papi sighed and explained how her blood always ran cooler than that of other Latin women, how her tongue craved milder, more catholic tastes. She was sick of being thought of as just another horny Puerto Rican girl. She wasn't even Puerto Rican, but most people never noticed the difference. *Cuban, Dominican, Latino, Hispanic* . . . She felt homeless in her tight-knit community, she wanted something bigger, more universal. That's why she started doing accents and practicing Santeria—those were the only other tools readily available. In Lulu she found a vessel, a body she could be born from. Born again from, anyway.

"You mustn't tell her, Henry."

Henry stared at his legs, thinking about Andy and Dr. Kiewicz.

Papi looked desperate. "I know a secret," she said. "I could give it to you. I could give you mine and you could give me yours. For keeps."

Henry looked up.

"It's about your father."

The Mozart didn't get much of a reaction from the Irukandji. Nor did the death metal, the James Brown, the whale sounds, the strobe light, nor proximity to fire, mirrors, nor surrounding the Kreisel tank with pictures of the Great Barrier Reef. Occasionally Henry's father would drop the temperature of the tank, let them feel the chill. Then he'd slowly warm it up, and as he did, he'd put pictures of himself against the glass. He wanted them to associate his image with something pleasant. Still, they ignored him.

This, he told himself, was the getting-to-know-ya stage. And while he was making progress, he wouldn't dare submerge any bare skin in the tank. That was his goal: recognition. To be able to swim, unscathed, among his fellow jellies. He wanted them to know him, to make the conscious decision *not* to kill him. Did they even know what killing was? They have advanced eyes, he reasoned, with lenses and retinas, and he'd surmised by trial and error that these supposedly brainless creatures have two separate stinging mechanisms: one that's intentional, one that isn't. They sting other animals but not rocks. They somehow know that rocks are inorganic. And they don't sting themselves or each other. "Promising," he noted in his logbook.

If all else failed, there were contingency plans. He could perhaps trick them into thinking he was a rock. Or even a fellow jelly. Or he could attempt to build up immunity to their sting by repeatedly injecting himself with the toxin. But these were last resorts. He wanted to be accepted, not to win by trickery.

On a Sunday morning he noticed a scuff on the Kreisel

and went looking in the basement for a chamois cloth. He found it in a closet on a stack of old board games: Sorry, Life, Risk. He opened Sorry and found a pad full of sketches signed by Henry. The first few were of legendary pirate flags: the flexed arm and sword of Thomas Tew; Bartholomew Roberts's captain and skeleton toasting to death; Blackbeard's devil holding an hourglass. Henry's father turned the pages. There were great big ships. Most striking was a meticulous rendition of the Royal Navy's single-masted Pirate Chaser, with billowy sails, stiff oars, and cannons. A seagull swooped low above the horizon. And in the lower left-hand corner there was a tiny bell-shaped monster that, if drawn to scale, would be about the size of a shaved baby carrot. Henry made the picture one day while Dad was out back washing the car. He used to sit and sketch the jellies as his mother did with him.

Henry's father looked long at the drawing, remembering how he used to tell Henry the story of the prominent Frenchman who died in Australia. He concentrated on the signature, lightly touching the letters, his letters — E-V-E-R-Y. Below the name there was a small self-portrait. He stared at it. He never knew his boy could draw.

After twenty minutes he took the book downstairs and showed it to the Irukandji.

"Look," he said, like a new dad talking to his baby. "That's you! That's a picture of *you*." The Cnidarian seemed taken by it. Henry's father pointed to the self-portrait. "And that's my boy," he said. "That's *my* boy."

The Irukandji hovered next to Henry, wagging its tentacles, almost touching the glass. *Miraculous!* Henry's father taped it to the tank and recorded the breakthrough in his logbook.

27

Page 2262: color-coded black for "hypocritical bastards, the lot of you!"

1/15/89

You walk around your whole life and you hear about the types of secrets that change a person's world. They're always big and ugly. A pretty secret isn't life-changing. Who really cares if you never knew that Aaron played a mean piano, or that deep down Charlie always loved to dance? It's the bad ones that will break you.

The word *motherfucker* has never seemed so literal. My father's not my father, his insides are inverted. My father's not my father, my father's dead. My father's not my father, he's just some guy my mother met on Martha's Vineyard, lied to, lived with for ten years, then left. My father's not my father and he doesn't even know it! I guess I'm not an Every, not a pirate, after all.

No, my father's not my father — he said he didn't love me unconditionally. He really did. He said that one night at the dinner table. He said, "Unconditional love is for suckers who are scared of being alone. If you love someone no matter what, you're missing what there really is to love them for. How could you love a person unconditionally? With all that we're capable of?"

I disagree when it comes to parents, and I'll tell you why. Nobody asks to be born. I guarantee if there's a land of unborn children the citizens aren't fighting over who gets to go next. Life is a gift — for *parents*. You people bring us here to fill your voids, you brand us with your *X*'s and your *Y*'s, your natures and your nurtures, and then you question our capabilities? You didn't have us for our sake — you had us for *yours*. You don't get credit for being nice to us. You're not a helluva person for giving things up. We answer your prayers, we make you feel productive and unselfish. We define you. We give you fresh starts and vessels to work out all your unfinished failures. We're here for *you*, because you asked for us, because you signed us up — without asking — for life! It's kidnapping, really. You better believe you're in it unconditionally. You want to be a helluva person? *Adopt.*

Oh, and don't worry about me, Mom and Dad, or whatever your names are. Don't worry, I'll keep the secret. I'll protect you both. I'll love *her* unconditionally instead. She'll fill my void to overflowing. Every little thing about her. Yeah, like the fact that she's very into celebrating other people's holidays — Chinese New Year, Walpurgisnacht, Maha Shiva Ratri — she really goes all out, like they *mean* something to her . . . and that she thinks tubas are just about the funniest things in the world — the way they look, the way they sound, even the word *tuba*. I'm only fifteen, but trust me, it's the tubas in life that'll get you through it. It's the tubas that'll keep you coming back for more.

Tomorrow we leave for the middle of the woods.

It took a while for Papi to convince Henry that keeping quiet about the Efram incident was ultimately for the greater good. For one thing, she said, he and Lulu weren't even related. But the clincher was the coins. After she told him the truth about his father, Papi handed Henry an old envelope filled with three quarter-sized tokens. "A present from Lulu," she said, still talking like her boss. "She told me to put them away somewhere, somewhere safe. 'I don't want you to touch 'em,' she told me. 'Put a *brick* on 'em. You know what a brick is? It's something *heavy*. And leave it there. Don't you touch 'em. And one day you're gonna be so happy.'"

Henry spilled the coins into his palm, which was still shaking from the news that he was a bastard. They were old-looking, dirty bronze, worth twenty-five cents on the face. He looked closely at the head in the center. There were eyes, a nose. It resembled . . . a smiling rat? Indeed, the rat was wearing a hat and bow tie. Above the hat it said, "Smile America, Say Chuck E. Cheese." On the back it said, "In Pizza We Trust." Henry put the coins back in the envelope and handed them to Papi.

"Chuck E. Cheese?"

"Her eyes aren't so good."

"No," said Henry.

"She thought they were precious. She thought they were precious and she gave them to *me*."

"They're for video games. Pinball, Skee-ball—"

"Worth a fortune," said Papi, swatting a tear before Henry could see it.

"They're worthless," said Henry.

Papi shook her head. "Not to me."

28

"I have a better idea."

They'd been living together for almost two weeks, and Harlan kept coming up with better ways to win the gold at AntFest. Competition suited and soothed him and he thought this particular victory would somehow mend his ruined marriage. He wanted to plant his toes behind an unsmudged starting line. He wasn't interested in talking about all the things they should've done or said—he wanted just to do them, say them, naturally, without it being seen as an attempt or an effort to make up for some past lapse or transgression. If he felt like washing the dishes, he'd wash the dishes. If he wanted to take an interest, he'd take an interest. This transition, he hoped, would be eased along by crushing the competition with the most sophisticated, spectacular terrarium these bug junkies had ever seen.

Hannah had already nixed the underwater idea. "We'd basically be waiting around for them to die," she said. "No way."

"That's okay," said Harlan, undeterred. "I have others."

"Do you?"

"Driver ants," he said. "We get a swarm of stinging driver

ants together in a big tank, a *massive* tank. I don't have to tell *you* this, but they'll line up at dawn in a huge row and advance, looking for food, any varmint that crosses their path — scorpions, tarantulas, birds, snakes, whatever — and at the end of the raid, in the afternoon, they'll bring the loot back to the bivouac."

She smiled when he said bivouac.

"Ants can pull up to fifty times their own body weight, yeah, so we'll show the assault. The lineup, the takedown, the drag-back. We'll put all these live animals in there — birds, rodents — and we'll watch them fall at the mandibles of the little guys. Strength in numbers. Triumph of the superorganism. We're gonna need a real big tank, though. You think maybe we could rent out a room? Or a field?"

His wife took no offense at his obvious attempt to use her hobby as a unifying force. She simply shrugged it off with a giggle.

"We could maybe show images of guerilla warfare in the background — Vietnam, the Zapatistas."

"I don't think so," she said.

"Okay then, what about the leaf-cutter? The leaf-cutter ant has been known to build a hill that's almost an acre wide."

"Yes," she said.

"And up to fifteen feet deep!"

"I was thinking smaller."

"Smaller than an ant hill?"

"What do you think about when you think about ants?"

"You," he said.

"About the *ants*."

"Work," he said. "The worker caste."

"What else?"

"Kinship. Community. They look out for each other."

She nodded.

"So?"

"So," she said, "everyone's always watching them work. Work, work, work. *Look at them build, look at them carry, look at them fight.* I wonder: You can take the ant out of the assembly line, but can you take the assembly line out of the ant? I want to see if we can get them to change their stripes."

Henry's father gave one of his nods. "How do we do that?"

"Luxury," she said. "We'll spoil them rotten. Give them everything they could possibly want."

29

The year before, the boys in Benna's family had camped out in the northern tier of Pennsylvania, a vast thicket of second-growth trees that stretches from the Catskill Mountains to the Allegheny National Forest. It's mostly scrub with an almost impenetrable lower story of stunted black birch, pine oak, hemlock, and vines that'll scratch a man's skin through his pants. That was the whole point. These outings weren't about lake swims and ghost stories and s'mores. No, said Benna, they were about *being men*. Benna's father chose unfriendly terrain and intentionally limited their provisions. It was a test—of strength, of character. This year the trip would take place in the inhospitable Pine Barrens of southern New Jersey, home to over a million acres of the largest unbroken wilderness east of the Mississippi, teeming with brackish water and copperheads.

Henry insisted they prepare for the worst. Benna snuck back to the Alcazar for supplies, most of which were now laid out on the bed in Lulu's guest room. She checked them off her list as she went:

long wooden matches, waterproof case
compass, map, rope, whistle, sheath knife,
    candles, flashlight
sleeping bag (eiderdown), extra socks (wool)
snakebite kit, antiseptic, aspirin, adhesive
    tape, and bandages
halazone tablets, vitamin pills, water
trail mix, jerky, jam, chocolate
freeze-dried astronaut snacks
rifle

It was Saturday, still dark out, just before dawn. Henry and Benna loaded their gear into the trunk of a taxi. The driver read the paper and ran the meter as the browsers, dressed in flannel, camouflage, and rubber-soled boots, waited for their targets to emerge from the Alcazar. Benna kept her eyes on the door; Henry tapped his tooth. The night before she'd told him a story about the Jersey Devil, a big-winged, cloven-hoofed, snake-bellied beast with the head of an angry horse. According to legend, she said, the Devil was to be the thirteenth child of one Mrs. Leeds, an indigent local shrew who, upon learning of her latest pregnancy, cried out, "Not another child! Let it be a devil!"

And so it was. Pushed from her womb in 1735, it whisked up the chimney and settled by a bog in the Pine Barrens where it has been feeding ever since on livestock and children. There have been hundreds of sightings over the years, and mobs of men have even stormed the woods with weapons. In 1951, a little boy said he saw the monster floating outside his bedroom window with blood dripping from its face. In 1966, a farmer blamed the Devil for eviscerating his entire stock of chickens—as well as the giant watchdogs there to protect them. Indeed, said Benna, it's widely known that seeing the Devil is the darkest of omens, a forecast of impending doom, and that members of the state police are each issued one silver bullet, just in case.

The story didn't scare Henry so much as depress him. He identified not with the mobs of men, but with the Leeds boy.

"Here they come!" said Benna, tapping the window of the taxi. Henry looked out and saw a man and a young man walking with purpose, dressed for survival. The man was in his forties and carried himself like a hero. "A superiority complex," said Benna. The young man looked about eighteen, moptopped and skinny, much less sure of himself. He was wearing a T&C Surf cap. Benna tapped the driver. "Follow them," she said. "Follow that Jeep, wherever it goes."

The cabbie put his paper on the passenger seat and followed the Jeep out of the city, onto the Garden State Parkway, toward Tuckerton. Henry thought the taxi looked funny on the highway.

After about forty-five miles, the Jeep pulled off near a dirt road. "Right there," said Benna, gesturing for the driver to pull over in the breakdown lane, a good distance behind the Jeep. "We'll get out there, right there." She tapped Henry. "Come on, Henry. We don't want to get too close."

For her sixteenth birthday, Gimmel got a nose job. Her parents scheduled the rhinoplasty five weeks in advance so she'd be sure to have her new nose on the big day. Jorden was arranging a surprise party at the roller-skating rink where Gimmel had celebrated her eleventh birthday. She was officially back together with Mope Pope, and he was furious at Jorden for doing such a nice thing.

"Makes me look bad," he said. "Besides, I don't skate."

Jorden didn't care how he looked—she didn't care if he dropped dead, and she told him as much. "Drop dead," she said when he vowed to ruin the party.

Gimmel was struggling through a period of intensive self-scrutiny, second-guessing everything from the shape of her hair follicles to the pitch of her voice to the topography of her face and body. She worried about the thickness of her ear-lobes, the space between her eyes, and most of all that she was just too big. Jorden had become a voracious reader of medical literature such as the *Journal of the American Medical Association* and the American Psychiatric Association's *Diagnostic and Statistical Manual of Mental Disorders* and her inchoate specialty covered a full range of body dysmorphic disorders. She thought Gimmel had a fine-looking nose, perfectly proportioned to her face. But she had no problem with a person taking whatever steps they felt were necessary to feel better.

Unfortunately, a week before the surprise party, over fries and shakes at Dotty's Dumpling Dowry, Gimmel said the steps she'd taken might have been in the wrong direction.

"I feel damaged." She was wearing an X-Ray Spex *Germ Free Adolescents* T-shirt, drinking her shake through a bendy straw, her nose pale purple and puffy.

"You look hot," said Jorden.

"Like I just went from mint condition to very good."

"Not at all—the other way around."

"You didn't like my nose before?"

"I liked your nose just fine before."

"But you just said it was the other way around."

"I don't like it when you're sad," said Jorden. "Makes your face sag."

"I know," said Gimmel, blushing. She dragged a fry through the ketchup. "I'm supposed to be looking *forward* to this whole sweet sixteen thing, right? Why aren't I?"

"You're being silly."

Gimmel smiled. She tended to fetishize her childhood—the smallness of everything—and liked it when people talked down to her. "Sixteen is a cusp, right? Mope Pope says it's a cusp."

"Everything's a cusp."

Gimmel held a fry like a cigarette between her fingers. "I think I have big fingers," she said. "I think I'm big-boned. Look at my finger compared to this fry."

"You're tall," said Jorden. "Everybody wants to be tall."

"*Boys* want to be tall. Girls want to be dainty. You're lucky, you're dainty in all the right places."

Jorden knew this to be true. She also knew that tall girls were less likely to get married than short girls. It's not so much that tall girls are less desirable, she'd learned, it's that men like to feel big. Of course, she kept such findings to herself.

"We should join a gym," said Gimmel. "The European Health Spa has everything—Nautilus, tanning stations, aerobics. They even do blood work. We could get AIDS tests."

"No more tests," said Jorden. Gimmel had taken to getting an AIDS test whenever she was feeling out of control or anxious about something. It was her coping mechanism. She'd had sex only with Mope Pope, and only about a dozen times, but she'd already had four tests. "Let's go to the movies later," said Jorden.

Gimmel let the fry dangle coolly from her lips. "You know the last time I went to the movies they didn't even ask me for an ID? They sold me an R-rated ticket and they didn't even ask me for proof."

"That's a compliment," said Jorden, remembering the time when she and Henry got thrown out of the Circle Cinema for sneaking into *Broadcast News*. She cupped her hand around her fist and pretended to light Gimmel's fry.

Gimmel puffed, exhaled, and blew the smoke into the sky. "Would you describe Mope Pope as solid? I know you think he's dull, and that I said he was a whole bunch of bad things, but at the end of the day, do you think he's down-to-earth?"

He's about as down-to-earth as the man in the moon, thought Jorden, but she'd never say such a thing. Gimmel was very protective of her man, and while she solicited opinions, it was clear she wanted support instead of truth. Jorden put a fry in her mouth and pretended to light it.

"He said maybe I could bind my hands, like a Chinese person. You know, like how they do with their feet? To make them smaller?"

Jorden wanted to tell Gimmel that nobody binds feet anymore, and that the Chinese government used to impose fines on the crazies who did it. But instead she ashed her fry in Gimmel's milkshake. Gimmel made a "how dare you!" face and ashed her fry in Jorden's milkshake. After the laughs died down, Gimmel asked Jorden if she missed Henry.

Jorden stayed quiet, took a final drag, and stubbed her fry out in a dollop of ketchup.

Benna's father and stepbrother walked stealthily through tangled vines, past pitcher plants and curly grass ferns. Henry was having a good time. He liked not seeing any people. The cold air tasted clean, and he found the stunted pygmy pines endearing.

1/17/89

I have to write fast because I'm not allowed to use any artificial light after dusk. It could give us away. Light also attracts mosquitoes, and I hate mosquitoes more than anything else in the world. Thankfully it's too cold for them now. I'd rather have a bed full of roaches. I really would. Benna said only girl mosquitoes bite and that made me happy to be a boy.

We haven't kissed once since we got to the woods this morning. We've been doing our best to remain invisible and that means being superaware of ourselves. That's the most important thing, and Benna's been very strict. *Don't get seen, don't get smelled, don't get heard.* "He's very aware," said Benna of her father.

As soon as we arrived, she showed me how much noise something very small can make. We crouched down and closed our eyes. She asked me if I heard the leaves rustling. I did. She asked me what I thought it was. At first I thought it was a deer. She said no, and then I thought it was a squirrel. Then I thought it was a field mouse or a chipmunk. Turns out it was a beetle. A big old beetle clomping through the leaves. "Imagine," she said, "what a person sounds like."

Still, I think we could kiss a little.

Anyway, we've been staying quiet, roughly sixty feet downwind from our targets at all times. Occasionally her father ducks out of sight and then minutes later reappears and ambushes his son, tackling him, rubbing his face in the dirt, stealing his sheath knife, and then critiquing his defensive skills. Benna and I walk behind a blind, a shield we made of pine, vine, and rope. We're wearing very good shoes, and warm, soft clothes — no Gore-Tex because it goes *sssh-sssh-sssh* when you walk. We carry fluffy pieces of pillow in case we need to muffle a sneeze or a cough. For eavesdropping, Benna brought a battery-operated Game Ear, which is really just a hearing aid for hunters. She could get only one, she said, which is fine with me — I have really terrific ears.

Last night, as we bundled into our sleeping bags on our tarp, we heard her dad telling his son some very standard man stuff about how we've all grown too accustomed to modern comfort and convenience, and how comfort is death. He kept referring to his son as "you people."

"You people think you don't have to know the skills, you don't have to learn the techniques," he said. "How to *cut*, how to *clean*, how to *kill* an animal. The best way is to stalk 'em. But when you stalk 'em, you gotta *trap* 'em and *catch* 'em. Getting close to a turkey doesn't get you a turkey. You gotta be able to *get* that turkey. Sure, you can sit up in a tree stand and plug a deer because it happens to walk under you. But to go out there and find that deer and kill that deer with primitive weapons — that's a feeling like no other."

He said to get a deer with a rock was pretty impossible. A spear? Improbable. A bow and arrow? Only if you're really good. "You get only one shot," he said, "so go for the vitals — heart, lungs. But let's say you *do* get it. Let's say she buckles. Now what? You people'd end up eating all the stuff you're not supposed to eat. You don't know about skinning or gutting, which organs are particularly nutritious and tasty and which should be thrown away."

The boy asked why they always had to hunt with Robin Hood–type bows and arrows. He knew his old man was against guns — "any idiot can drop a buck with a slug and a scope," he'd said — but what about using a better bow?

"Man's been using longbows for ten thousand years," said

his father. "At the Battle of Agincourt, the English defeated an army four times its size using longbows. You want to use a compound bow, you might as well just go right to the grocery store." He took out his bow, made of fine-grained yew with rattlesnake skin backing—a present, said Benna, from her. She gave it to him for his fortieth birthday, hoping it would effectively soften his no-girls-allowed policy. It hadn't.

"Takes a big, strong man to pull a nice English longbow," he had told her. "To aim right, hold it, and make a good, accurate shot. Are you a big, strong man?"

"That's one of the few things I can't do," Benna told me. "I can't pull a bow by myself." I'd seen her cut steak, climb a rope, tie a necktie. She showed me how she puts the top of the nail polish bottle in the crook of her right arm and runs each finger across the brush. Now she watched, doe-eyed, as her father handed the bow to his son.

Gimmel was always allowed to stay home from school on her birthday. She'd have breakfast in bed, pad around the house, maybe go shopping or watch TV. She was born at six o'clock in the morning. It was almost nine and Mope Pope hadn't called.

"He's at school," said Gimmel's mother.

"Payphones?" said Gimmel.

Jorden called at nine-thirty from a payphone at the roller-skating rink. She was decorating the place entirely with Mylar balloons and Hello Kitty favors (Gimmel's childhood favorite). The cake was a giant Hello Kitty, and in the goody bags were Hello Kitty key chains and stickers, a box of Nerds, a tube of glitter, puffy paint, and a trial-size bottle of Jean Naté bath gel.

"Hello, Kitty!" said Jorden. She enjoyed dropping small hints about the surprise party. "Happy birthday!"

"Thanks." Gimmel sounded gloomy. "Where are you?"

"What do you mean?" Jorden lied. "School."

"Have you seen Mope Pope? I haven't heard from him. I've been sixteen for more than three hours and I still haven't heard from him."

"He's probably thinking of the perfect thing to say."

"When did everything get so big?" said Gimmel. "Remember eleven? Remember how little everything was?"

"I remember eleven."

"Eleven was good. Probably the last good birthday."

"You're just a cub," said Jorden. "Statistically speaking, you have four more sixteen-year spans to go."

The manager approached her with a question about how curly to make the streamers. Jorden covered the phone, held up her index finger: *one second*. "Okay, honey, I gotta run to gym now."

"Hit a grand slam for me."

"We're still going skating tonight, right?"

"Yeah, but I'm wearing pants. I tried on that little mini again and there's no way I'm wearing it. I look like a sofa."

Jorden laughed. "I'll wear pants, too, then. Happy birthday, kiddo."

"Thanks. And if you see Mope Pope, tell him to call his girlfriend. Don't tell him to call Gimmel, tell him to call his *girlfriend*. Okay?"

Jorden hung up and started curling streamers with a scissors. The manager offered to help but she wanted them all to be curled just right. By one o'clock, the Hello Kitty plates, cups, and napkins were set up on the buffet bar. Jorden ordered the appetizers and wrote out a list of Gimmel's favorite songs for the DJ.

Meanwhile, at school, the ninth grade theater class was about to get a crash course in melodrama. They were supposed to convene in the gym for a lesson on Broadway dance choreography. Instead, as they walked through the doors they were unwittingly turned into a tragic chorus. Mope Pope was dangling from the rafters, a rope cinched tight around his purple neck. He was wearing a black T-shirt that said "Atrocity Exhibition." He died with his boots on, his perfect hair pulled back in a wispless ponytail.

Gimmel was nine hours into her seventeenth year when she turned on the TV and saw Alton Hauser broadcasting live from the front of her high school. She caught the end of his report: "And unlike the theme song to one of America's most popular television shows, it's been made clear *once again* to this suburban community that suicide is most assuredly *not* painless." The segment closed with a zoom in on a piece of graffiti written in white paint on the Dumpster in the back of the school: "Mope Pope Lives."

Gimmel recognized his writing. For the first time in her life, all the red rushed from her face.

Across town, Jorden was just about finished. She put up a sign-in board on an easel by the entrance of the rink. In the center was a picture of eleven-year-old Gimmel in a little blue skirt and tights, her skates slung over her shoulder. Jorden was the first to sign the board. "Eliminate the ought," she wrote. It was her own adaptation of "to thine own self be true." "Happy birthday, kiddo!"

She put the cap back on the silver paint pen, said "See ya later" to the manager, and biked home to get ready for the party.

Her dad was on the farmer's porch when she got there. He was drinking mineral water, dressed in an Adidas warm-up suit. His skin looked taut; he'd just returned from a jog. He was in the process of transforming himself into a fitness man. According to his analyst, Jorden was passively responsible for the bulimia. As Daughter grew and prospered, Father shrunk and retreated, binged and purged—"An attempt," he said, "to stop the world from spinning. I could actually feel it, like I was on a treadmill. Everything was fast-forwarding out of control."

Together, he and Jorden worked out a regimen to reroute his compulsions. He chose a sport. Not to root for, to play. He became obsessed with time control, punctuality, efficiency. He went from eating mayonnaise and wearing smocks to eating seaweed and wearing a stopwatch. The roof rats were gone, the malted chocolate milk was back in the refrigerator. Not that he'd touch the stuff. Too much saturated fat.

"Hi, Dad," said Jorden, flipping the kickstand with her foot.

"Hey," said her dad. He pushed the start button on his stopwatch.

She walked up onto the porch. "Good run?"

"Yeah," he said, sticking his finger in the water bottle.

"What's wrong?"

He checked his pulse.

"What happened?" She braced herself. "Are you okay? Is Henry okay?"

"Henry's fine," said her dad. "I'm fine." He pushed stop on the watch and told her about Mope Pope.

Jorden got back on her bike, pedaled hard toward the roller-skating rink, and took down all the perfectly curled streamers. She called Gimmel from the payphone. Her mom said she was out getting an AIDS test.

30

Only two days had passed since Henry first stepped into the wild, but already he'd grown accustomed to its temperament: the flow of the streams, the sound of the tree frogs, the un-selfish way in which a pine stood still even as an animal—a beaver, perhaps—gnawed on its trunk. He'd quickly learned a bobcat's tracks from a fox's, the sex of a turkey by the tone of its call. With a pinch of sand he could tell the way of the wind. He could spot the white tail of a deer through the pines, and when he did, he saw a more ordered version of the universe—he thought not of a cuddly cartoon, but of the tender back straps running down either side of its spine, and of the protein, fat, and vitamins they contained. He'd watched as Benna's father and his son pushed hooks through the tendons of one such doe, hung her upside down, cut off her tail, peeled her hide down over her face, severed her esophagus, removed her entrails, and quartered the animal with a knife. It looked like a drawing in a science book—all muscle. More significantly, it looked like food.

And yet, despite this sense of oneness with his newfound yet ancient cohabitants, he felt as if his dearest ally was slipping into a swamp. Benna had turned cold, steering her mouth away from his, veering instead toward the other men in her life.

Henry was getting annoyed. He knew they were "on the browse" and that the stakes were unusually high. But he'd pictured his girl above him, biting her fluffy piece of pillow to keep from getting seen, getting smelled, getting heard. And yet—nothing. Not even a head pat. Until deep into their second night when Benna flirtatiously wagged a surprise in a way that reminded Henry of a civilization beyond the woods in which man hunts woman with primitive weapons through all seasons and with no daily bag limits.

Benna pulled the cork. "Bourbon?"

They passed the bottle back and forth, the cold air getting warmer with each swig. They didn't talk but there were sounds. Henry unzipped his sleeping bag. Benna unzipped her pants. They both kept their hands covered: Henry wore gloves, Benna wore one glove and two heavy wool elastic socks.

Hours later, Henry awoke to a shriek in the distance. His nose was freezing. Polaris was due north in the sky. Benna was snoring, still wearing her socks and glove. He slid out from under her and found the bourbon just where he'd tossed it a few hours earlier. He took a sip. Then a gulp. The shriek came back louder, and in addition to the liquor, there was fear in Henry's belly. He felt around for the Savage rifle that Benna had bought off one of the bellboys at the Alcazar. There was a bullet in the chamber; Henry clicked off the safety. He skulked about, patrolling the perimeter, squinting as if that would help him see through the black. He took another sip of bourbon, went "Aaahhh" as he swallowed. The shrieks were getting closer, about twenty yards away, over by Benna's father's camp.

Henry crept, the rifle perpendicular to his body, his finger on the trigger. *My footsteps are much louder than a beetle's,* he thought. *My heart is much larger than a turkey's. Thump-thump. Thump-thump.* It reminded him of the thump on Benna's door, before he was banished to the tub, and of the awkward way she greeted him in the hallway at the Alcazar, dressed as Death. He took a few more steps and another gulp of bourbon. He started thinking about the Ettinger reunion, but his flashback of the pretty phantom was interrupted by a flapping sound.

Henry jumped. Something swooped above his head. He held the weapon with both hands, jerked it from side to side, up, down, the barrel bouncing from nothing to nothing. It was dark and more dark and that's what made the eyes so startling. They were white-hot, bloody, inches from his face. The Devil's eyes.

Henry dropped the bourbon and fired — *kapow* — the kick sending him to the ground, his head hitting a stone.

Then silence. The shrieking was replaced by the nasal honks of tree frogs, and Henry, dreaming back to when Stega Tunguska KO'd the Enforcer, slowly passed out, hugging the rifle like he used to hug Moo.

As the stars blended in with the dawn, he woke up choking. There was a heavy boot against his chest, a broadhead arrow aimed directly at his vitals.

31

Hannah sat up in her old bedroom. It was a different bed (smaller, harder) in a different place (the back corner instead of the left wall). She noticed every change—a feat because everything had changed. Some things, like the bed and the dresser, had got smaller. Others, like the TV and the pillows, had grown. The floral wallpaper had been stripped, replaced by sea-colored paint. She hated paint. Her husband knew this, of course.

Harlan was in the driveway with the snowblower. It was mid-April, but they'd gotten a few inches the night before. She had once naively suggested putting some sort of heating rods beneath the pavement, but he said, "No, that's idiotic, it's just snow." And he enjoyed removing it.

Hannah thought of metaphors as she looked out the window. All the common ones crossed her mind: innocence, blankness, beauty, and the impermanence of these things. She thought of how, in all those frosty inches, there weren't two snowflakes alike. But it was the inches themselves that consumed her. The *accumulation*. She liked saying the word, but it made her feel old. She thought of all the things she'd accumulated, all the things she'd lost. Henry wrote, "Life is the accumulation of masks and heirs." Hannah picked up the ledger. *How did I become the heir to this?*

Outside she heard the hum of the snowblower. She opened the window. She used to like watching Harlan clear the driveway. He looked sturdy out there, dressed in a parka, hat, gloves, and boots. He worked well with the machine. It was methodical, geometric, the black of the driveway exposed one strip at a time.

Hannah opened the ledger and flipped to one of her favorite entries, a poem logged in the February of Henry's final year.

> *To sit inside and watch the snow*
> *I think, therefore, I think I know*
> *I've had dreams, I've seen the show*
> *Perhaps a girl I used to know*
> *Unique as any flake of snow*
> *The streets are plowed so off I go*
> *To see the ground or is me woe?*
> *To see the ground or is me woe?*

She read the poem twice, not that she needed to. She'd read it hundreds of times and could easily recite it from memory. But she liked looking at his writing, picturing his hand as he wrote it. Now she saw another meaning in the last two lines. It had always seemed clear to her that "the ground" was truth, and no matter how beautiful the covering, you'd be "woe" not to see it. But now she read it differently. Perhaps the "woe" comes from *seeing* the ground. Perhaps there are times when it's better not to see it. Perhaps the snow can sometimes be a blessing. Is that why Henry chose never to confront her about leaving him? About lying?

Cold air filled the bedroom. The inches in the driveway were diminishing. Hannah held the ledger like a tablet against her chest. "You're his father," she said, looking at Harlan, her breath fogging the window. "You're his dad."

Harlan had not yet discovered the truth, but she could tell by the bookmark that it was just a matter of days. She scoured the pages, quickly tearing out any references to this particular "ground."

This, she thought, *is what Henry would have wanted. This,* she thought, *is for the greater good.*

Outside another strip of snow turned black beneath the blower.

When he finished the driveway, Harlan kicked his boots against the stone wall by the basement door. He tossed his hat and gloves on a shelf and hung his parka on a hook. He was red-faced and sweaty; his hands itched. Henry never shared his father's fondness for household tasks—he didn't care if the door knocker was shiny, or if the dead leaves piled up on the lawn. But the old man had a craftsman's passion for the menial.

He could smell the hot chocolate as he made his way up the basement stairs. Harlan called it *hot chocolate;* Hannah called it *cocoa.* Cocoa sounded so much better, he thought, but he felt funny saying it, like it was affected, or European. He felt the same way about *flapjacks* and *porridge.* He'd always just say *pancakes* and *hot cereal.*

"For my yardman," said Hannah, holding out a mug topped with marshmallow fluff, just how he liked it.

"Any booze in here?"

"Later," she said. "We have work to do." She was preparing brunch for the ants. On the menu today: a baby fly (dead, diced) drizzled with honey and a side of dandelion seeds. For dessert, a shard of a cherry Jolly Rancher.

Harlan followed his wife into the playroom, where they'd set up the terrarium. There hadn't been any jellies in the house since the funeral. He watched the ants crawl furiously over rotting tree bark. He watched them communicate, he watched them look out for each other.

Go to the ant, thou sluggard; consider her ways and be wise.

He thought of his final experiment with the jellyfish, the most promising since taping up the self-portrait of Henry. He'd been adding a microdose of fentanyl into the water just before sticking his bare finger in up to the nail. He'd suck on his finger, wipe it under his armpit—anything to get his *self* in there. The hope was that the Irukandji would comprehend a trigger effect. When his skin entered the water—bliss.

As he stood next to his wife, looking down at the unspoiled ants in their split-level luxury terrarium, he wondered: *Was I heartless, spineless, brainless? A deadly passive drifter who accidentally bumped into my boy?*

"You know," said his wife, squeezing his hand, "honey ants store extra nectar in their bellies, and if one of their friends is hungry, they'll throw up into their mouth."

Henry's father comprehended a trigger effect. When her hand squeezed his—bliss.

32

Page 2438: color-coded blue

3/1/89

The nightmares persist, unshakable, every one of them *to be continued*. Last night her neck unzipped, revealing a state-of-the-art voice box and a wrinkled tongue that hung like flypaper. She had no lips, only teeth. No eyelids, no fingers, no fur. Her face was the farthest thing from frank. Her skin was rough and cold and waterproof. She wouldn't stop dancing.

I'm still spooked by what happened in the Pine Barrens, unable to see the forest for the trees — a saying, by the way, that I never really appreciated until entering the woods.

The Devil, of course, was no devil, but a massive great blue heron, a fifty-five-inch bird with blue-gray wings that spread up to six feet. It's a really terrific bird. At least it was before I shot it point blank in the face, right through the beak.

My "father" always said, "Burn me once, shame on you. Burn me twice, shame on me." One time he even said that to a bottle of gin. He said he hated when people blamed the alcohol, like that's any excuse. Well, I'll have to respectfully disagree. Drunk people can do some pretty stupid things. I don't think I would have shot that bird if I hadn't drunk all that bourbon. I don't think I would have thought it was the stupid Jersey Devil, and I don't think I would've ever believed in Benna in the first place. Apparently it doesn't take just alcohol to get drunk; you can get drunk on a whole bunch of things. The heart sneaks up on you, the brain produces juices that produce emotions, and before you know what happened you're acting corny, buying bananas. It's all very chemical.

Which is not to say that I don't take full responsibility. I feel really bad. You should have seen the looks on their faces. It was dark out there, but still. You could tell that they were reassessing, rewriting their histories, reshaping their futures. Picture it: Benna, her father, and her stepbrother are all sleeping. They hear a rifle blast, cautiously approach the scene, and find a drunk teenager passed out hugging a gun next to a giant dead bird. And then they see each other. Talk about shrieks. I don't know who was more surprised. It was horrifying. Sure, he may have been a crappy dad, but when the spy is discovered spying, well, that's as unforgivable an act as any.

And I feel bad about the bird. Not as bad as I would have had I not plucked off its feathers, lopped off its head, tail, and feet, and slow-cooked it over a campfire. There wasn't a lot of meat at all, the legs were pretty tough, almost inedible, but the breast wasn't too bad. Anyway, I felt a whole lot better after eating it. I even finger-painted some of its blood on my face as a sign of peace and respect. That's what the Indians used to do. Something about Mother Earth and the Great Spirit and the life cycle. And as I sat there, alone, abandoned, my stomach filled with one of my old feathered foes, I thought back to an earlier revelation. *Me and a girl in a room — that's it, that's everything.* Yeah, maybe if you never leave the room. Maybe if you never see the forest for the trees.

Truth is, a lot of that stuff I wrote about Benna wasn't even true. I was filling up the vessel, putting words into her mouth, loving something unconditionally.

Olly-olly-oxen-free! Come out, come out, wherever you are!

Okay, so she never said anything to me about tubas. She never opened up the window, pointed to a star, and said, "That's how far away I feel from you right now." We did look our names up in the phone book, though, and we did make an igloo out of all those extra pillows. And she was very good at sex. And she did like to pee at the same time as me, that was true. She was really pretty wonderful with Lulu, and she had a very legitimate reason for changing her name. But we never called each other Roo and Joey. She never said, "Roo, I miss your pouch." She didn't even *like* me that much. We were always in costume, how could she? All the magic was just *magic.* Smoke and mirrors, a bluff. I ignored the warning signs; I planted all those good things because those were the things I dreamed of when I dreamed about a girl — my sleepy seeds, if you will. What a nightmare.

Turns out she was dating Split Jimmy the whole time. He was the one who'd kissed her lips that first night. He was the one who got to lie next to her on New Year's Eve. Benna liked me, sure, I guess, but she really just wanted me to go with her into the woods. That's what she told me before telling me to never speak to her again. She even spit at me, which is almost as bad as getting shot. Believe me, getting spit on is the worst.

Love can conquer anything except for lack of love. Jorden

said that. She was right, of course. About everything. Benna's missing hand was the earth and I revolved around it.

Jorden's the one that likes tubas. Jorden's the one who celebrates other people's holidays.

I'm more confused than ever. More out of place. I'm really in a bad way. Back on the browse. I don't whistle, not even sad songs. I feel drastic. Today I heard a man get crushed by a subway train. I didn't see it happen, I just heard the sound: a helpless yelp cut short by a slow crash, then silence. The silence was part of the sound. The driver seemed tense, almost defensive, you could tell by the way he smoked his cigarette — quick drags pushed hard through his nose, right down to the filter. "I didn't see a thing," he said. "I just heard this sort of dull crunch. It didn't feel like a person. Not that I'd know what a person feels like."

Who am I? What a question! I considered changing my name, fleeing the nation, joining a subculture or a minority. But which? I called Dr. Adam Kiewicz to find out how I could turn myself into a paraplegic. I made my voice sound deep so he wouldn't know I was a kid. We discussed all sorts of methods at length. He kept saying, "Hypothetically, of course . . ."

I thought the operation would have involved some sort of banging with a blunt instrument like a hammer or an ax or maybe even a gunshot, but it was actually much more scientifically sound and involved something called the Seldinger technique. Through the use of tiny catheters and polyvinyl alcohol Dr. Kiewicz said he would have much more control over the operation, and the recovery period would be days instead of months. I'd lie back on an operating table. A live feed of my insides would be broadcast on a monitor.

To dull the edge, a nurse would deliver fifty micrograms of fentanyl into my arm. To numb the entrance site she'd inject five cc's of lidocaine in the crease of my groin. Then the doctor would stick my beating right femoral artery with a needle, through which he'd thread a wire. He'd pull out the needle, leaving the wire, then slide a plastic sheath over the wire. Through that sheath he'd thread the catheters. Then he'd inject a contrast dye so he could track which arteries fed which parts of my spinal cord. He'd maneuver the catheters through my central nervous system, knocking off sections of the cord by injecting polyvinyl alcohol into the appropriate arteries. "This stuff's like liquid buckshot," he explained. "Lots of tiny little round things that go in and block the vessels. As soon as they hit, you'll feel it. It'll creep up your body. You'll lose sensation in your toes, then your feet, then your legs. The alcohol not only blocks the vessel, it kills the tissue. Now, the human body will always try to heal itself," he said. "You kill a certain artery and some other artery will open up and try to supply blood to the damaged area —"

That's very nice of those arteries, I thought. *Looking out for each other like that. Helping out even though it won't help.*

As Dr. Kiewicz talked of dead tissue, I started thinking about the jellyfish's nematocysts and of that prominent Frenchman who died in Australia. But most of all I thought of Jorden, her brain, her unpierced ears, and how even an x-ray could never really show who she is on the inside or the outside. She always said she had no problem with a person taking whatever steps they thought were necessary to better themselves. I wonder how she'd feel about this.

33

In addition to the nose job, Gimmel got a membership to the European Health Spa for her birthday. Her parents bought her the extra present because of what happened to Mope Pope.

"Nothing *happened* to Mope Pope," said Jorden. She was sitting with Gimmel in the pale yellow locker room of the spa. They were both wrapped in pink towels. Jorden had just come from the sauna. Gimmel had just finished a full-body tanning session—she thought a golden glow would make her blushing less conspicuous. She was feeling better because her AIDS test had come back negative.

"No note, nothing," said Gimmel, looking in the mirror. "Jesus, I'm red." She touched her cheeks, her forehead. She really was red.

"It'll turn," said Jorden. "By tomorrow afternoon, it'll turn." She wondered what would happen if Gimmel blushed.

"I'm not gonna go looking for all the warning signs," said Gimmel, turning away from the mirror. "I'm not gonna go beating myself up."

"Who said you should?"

"His mother called my mother. She asked if I'd noticed anything strange lately. Any *hints*. She said I spent the most time with him so if anyone should've reported the strange stuff it was me."

"She's just reaching," said Jorden.

"*Reported?* What was I supposed to do, call her up and be, like, 'Excuse me, but your son's obsessed with his legacy, and by the way, it really turns him on to touch my calves'?"

Jorden checked out Gimmel's calves. "It did?"

"Let me ask you something: When did it become deep to be bored? He was always saying how bored he was, how *empty* everything was. As if being bored means you're so aware of all the other possibilities, all the things you *could* be doing. Like what? What are you gonna do? *Kill* yourself?" She was getting pretty worked up. "I mean it's not as if he was tortured or anything, right?" She slowed down, shaking her head, almost in tears. "I don't think he was. I don't think he was tortured."

Jorden shrugged. She hadn't told her yet about the surprise party.

Gimmel stared at her hands: the backs of her fingers, the grooves in her palms. She fiddled with a cuticle. "I don't," she said, hanging her head, making a sad, defeated fist. "Not at all."

Jorden put her hand on top of Gimmel's. She tucked a wisp of hair behind her ear. "What, kiddo?"

"I don't expect anything."

Jorden liked Gimmel. She had good taste in music, she was fun to shop with, she said funny things sometimes. But Jorden knew they wouldn't still be speaking twenty years from now. It wouldn't end badly, it would just end.

"Maybe he's better off," said Gimmel, pulling her fist away.

"Maybe he got what he wanted. There's something to be said for that, isn't there? Getting what you want?" Gimmel went to the mirror and covered her skin with a layer of cream.

That night, Jorden called Henry at the Alcazar. She hadn't written in a while, but now she had something important to say. The lady at the front desk said he'd checked out, and no, she didn't know where he had gone.

34

Papi sat by the foot of the canopy bed and studied her sleeping boss's open mouth. According to the doctor, it would never again utter a coherent word. During the night, Lulu had suffered an ischemic stroke. "The result of which, in this particular case, is something called expressive aphasia," said her doctor, a solemn man with a gray mustache. "It's quite possible she'll be able to hear and perhaps even understand you. But she'll never speak again."

"We had a conversation last night," protested Papi, her voice still sounding like Lulu's. "Just last night."

"Did she complain at all? Headache? Dizziness? Was anything numb?"

Papi felt numb. She had a headache. She was dizzy.

"Are you okay?" said the doctor.

"She told me to keep quiet," said Papi, as if she'd overlooked a significant hint. "She said, 'Keep quiet, Papi.' She never said that to me before. I was always saying that to her. 'Keep quiet, Lulu.' She used to say that was going to be the title of my biography."

Papi stared at Lulu's mouth and wondered if by some mutant strain of Santeria she'd accidentally stolen her voice.

The day before, the women had been drinking piña coladas on the roof deck since the early afternoon. That morning, Lulu had attended a bris; Papi's best friend had her second abortion.

"I'm aging," said Lulu, staring into the Hudson. "Look at me. I'm not *me* anymore. I look in the mirror and I see someone else."

Papi twirled her drink umbrella between her fingers. "You're getting older."

"I know I'm getting older. Don't you think I know I'm getting older?"

"I am, too," said Papi, an attempt to help shoulder the load.

Lulu tossed her maraschino cherry over the edge of the building. She looked at Papi, jealous of the keratin in her hair, the collagen in her skin. "I used to have the most *wonderful* hair. People would stop me on the street—strangers—to tell me how much they liked it."

Papi nodded. She'd seen the pictures.

"You know what the worst thing is? It isn't being old and feeling old. That wouldn't be so bad. You'd come to terms. There'd at least be symmetry. No, the worst thing—the very worst thing—is to be old and feel young." Lulu looked toward the Hudson. "You ever hear the saying 'too late for the Follies'?"

Now, the doctor took a pad from his coat pocket and wrote down a few emergency phone numbers. The Betty Boop brooch sparkled on Lulu's hope chest. Papi stared at her boss on the bed. She was sleeping, wigless. Her head looked like a coconut—small, wispy, crackable. *Darle coco al santo,* thought Papi, as she tried to push thoughts of coffins from her mind.

The doctor handed her a prescription for blood-thinner. When he stood up to go, Papi stood up too. Like the mother of a newborn, she was scared to be left in charge. "What do you mean she'll never speak again?"

"She can make noises," said the doctor, putting on his cashmere scarf. It was early March but the forecast called for snow. "Word salad, they call it."

"How will I know what she means?"

The doctor spoke slowly. "The part of her brain, the one that controls speech, is dead. It's called an infarction. She knows it's dead, she understands that she can't speak. And she'll be frustrated because of it. She'll babble, maybe, or groan a little. Or talk nonsense. She might choose to write things down. You'll have to figure out her new voice." He tightened his scarf.

"Lulu loved cashmere," said Papi.

"She still does," he said reassuringly. He put on his leather gloves before touching the doorknob. "Goodbye, Papi."

"See you later," she said softly, waving, bending her wrist up and down like the top of a crocodile mouth. She listened to his footsteps as he walked away, then went over to the window. It was snowing. *Goodbye, Papi.* She watched the doctor hail a taxi and wondered what his home looked like, if he wiped his feet before entering. She wondered with whom he lived, if they ever got sick. She wondered if anyone knew him like an x-ray.

Papi lit the candles in the fireplace and walked around in her purple silk mules. It was payalaya night. She sat in the high-backed red chair and tried to get comfortable, but every position felt wrong. "Are you hungry?" she called out, but there was no answer. Lulu was resting. "It's payalaya night,

Lulu, come on!" Papi went into the kitchen, put on her red-checkered apron, heated up the skillet, and began to cook. "I'm leaving all my secret ingredients right out on the counter!"

As Papi cut the sausage into half-moon wedges, the phone rang.

"Hello?"

"Lulu!" said the voice on the other end. "F-Man here. Waddaya say there, baby?"

Papi stared out the window. It was really coming down, white chalk sketches across the streetlights. As a kid, she'd throw stones at the bulbs, hoping for a blackout.

"Lulu?"

The snow was accumulating; she could barely see the ground.

"Lulu?"

Papi kept quiet. She looked down and saw Henry making his way across the street. She could tell he was coming to say goodbye.

"Hello?"

Papi pressed her fingers to the pane, leaving prints.

35

Jorden's dad was wearing sweatbands and a fleece-lined nylon warm-up suit, stretching his hamstrings on the farmer's porch. It was March 21, 1989, chilly for the first day of spring.

Henry walked up the steps. "Hiya!"

"Every, m'boy!" The exclamation point was back. He looked healthy, like a man who'd found what he'd been looking for. They shook hands, firmly, like equals. Henry thought about hugging him, but Jorden's dad didn't make the move, so Henry didn't either.

"Looks like you chose a sport," said Henry.

"I started a jogging club. For marathoners." He was a body man now, in training, passionate about his physicality. *Blood pressure, heart rate, minutes per mile.* "I've been eating kelp," he said, fiddling with his stopwatch.

"Jorden still rooting for baseball?"

"She's been waiting for you to come home."

"Really?"

"Don't tell her I told you that."

"I won't," said Henry. "I've been waiting to come home, too."

"Choose a sport yet?"

"I did," said Henry, pulling an imaginary bow, closing his right eye. "Bow hunting."

Jorden's dad smiled and hit start on his stopwatch. There was a glint of that old "gather 'round" look in his eye. "She's at the bike rack."

Henry put his hands in his pockets and took the five-minute walk to his old school. The bike rack looked older, rustier. A few of the bars were missing. He walked over to the front steps and noticed for the first time that there was no handicapped ramp.

A voice behind him said, "The Every boy."

Henry turned around. It was Jorden. Her eyes looked rounder. She was wearing a light blue windbreaker and holding her favorite juggling balls. Six of them, all different colors.

"Any new tricks?"

She began tossing and catching all six balls, a feat she'd previously deemed "too advanced." She was marvelous. But right in the middle she stepped back and let the balls fall like a muffled drum roll. "Henry?"

"Yes."

"What are you doing here?"

Henry reached into his back pocket and handed her a card with a large sombrero on it. Inside it said "Happy Benito Juarez Day!"

Jorden checked the date on her calculator watch. So it was: The national holiday in honor of Mexico's most beloved leader. Last year they'd celebrated with a couple of tacos. "Happy Benito Juarez Day to you, too," she said.

"I was thinking maybe we could get some flan. At the cake place."

"They have flan at the cake place?"

Henry pulled out a roll of quarters. Jorden felt like punching him, bruising him, but she couldn't help but smile.

They held hands as they walked. The kerchiefed woman behind the counter at the cake place said, "No flan," so Jorden ordered a piece of lemon sponge. Henry ordered a cinnamon bun with extra icing. They paid in quarters and took their treats back to the bike rack, where they assumed their old position: she leaning against the bars, he with his head in her lap.

"Adam Kiewicz?" Jorden twirled his hair as she spoke. "That's the name of the surgeon you spoke to? Adam Kiewicz?"

"Yeah," said Henry.

"The Adamkiewicz artery is the largest blood vessel that feeds the spinal cord."

"How do you know that?"

Jorden shrugged. "Just do."

"Could we still eat meals together? Even if I was a paraplegic?"

"We could, but if you did that to yourself I would never help you. I wouldn't push you in your chair. We could be at the foot of Heartbreak Hill and I still wouldn't push you."

"It was a silly idea," said Henry, remembering Split Jimmy's horns.

"Mope Pope used to get aroused by squeezing Gimmel's calves."

"Why?"

"I don't know. He killed himself."

Henry sat up. He thought of Teddy Rabian and Alton Hauser. "Why?"

"He was trying to ruin my party. I was throwing a surprise party for Gimmel and he didn't want to look bad so he said he was going to ruin it, and then he did."

"That's the reason?"

"I'm sure there were others. There must've been others." She pointed to the wall beyond the bike rack. In white spray paint it said MOPE POPE LIVES. "Those are all over town."

"How'd he do it?"

"Hung himself in the gym. The drama class found him."

"You were right," said Henry. "Suburban boys are best at it. How's Gimmel?"

"Not so good. She joined the European Health Spa."

Henry pulled bunches of blades from the lawn.

"Have you been home yet?" said Jorden. "Have you seen your dad?"

"There's something I need to do first," said Henry. "Will you help me?"

Henry hadn't been home since just after Thanksgiving. He and Jorden scoped out the place from a neighbor's yard. It looked smaller, more provincial. But everything was where it belonged.

"My final browse," said Henry.

"Operation Irukandji," said Jorden.

The plan was simple. Get inside (easy — Henry had a key). Free the Irukandji from its cage (risky — possible death by envenomation). Return it to its natural environment (Henry knew the perfect beach where there was a boat). Jorden agreed to bend her no-stealing policy on account of this being more about "returning property to its rightful owner."

It was almost dinnertime. Henry and Jorden watched as the light in the kitchen went out. The electric garage door went up. As usual, Henry's father was off to the Rotisserie for half a chicken and two sides: macaroni and cheese and creamed garlic spinach.

Jorden set the walkie-talkies; she was the lookout. Henry scuttled across the street in a crouched position. He opened the door with the key, a large piece of Tupperware tucked under his arm. He went straight to his former playroom, pulled on the protective gloves, and took the net off the wall. The Kreisel tank glowed blue in the dark, making gurgling sounds. He peered over the top and took a long look at his old pal, remembering their times together. "I'm back now, jelly," he said.

The screen was easy to lift. Henry put the Tupperware next to the edge, and with the net, made the transfer. As he was closing the lid—

"Abort!" yelled Jorden through the walkie-talkie. Henry's father was coming back. "Abort! Get out!"

Henry heard the front door open. There was no place to hide.

Jorden sprinted over to the house and stood watching, helpless, through the playroom window. Henry cowered in the corner. He watched his father walk straight into the kitchen and rifle through the menu drawer. He quickly found what he'd come for. A coupon for the Rotisserie. He shut off the light and went back out the front door.

Jorden's dad was sleeping when they got home. He went to bed very early these days, right after a macrobiotic meal.

Henry put the Tupperware in the upstairs bathroom and collapsed next to Jorden on her bed. In the morning they planned on catching the bus to Tenean Beach.

"That was close," said Jorden, taking off her shoes and socks.

"You were great," said Henry.

"Partners," she said, squeezing his hand.

"You're always great." Henry paused to reconsider his statement. "Talk about an overused word, right? I could come up with another word, a more specific, less-used word, but it would just be another word. You know what I mean, though, right? Sometimes I don't know if you know what I mean."

Jorden touched his leg. "If you were a paraplegic you wouldn't be able to feel this."

"No," said Henry.

She went higher. "Or this."

He smiled. "Nothing."

"Or even here?" She was in the crease of his groin.

"Not really," said Henry, but his body disagreed.

"Not *really?*"

"You know," said Henry, "that first night with Moo—I was thinking about you. I was thinking about us when it happened."

Jorden climbed on top of him. "I called you at the Alcazar last week. They said they didn't know where you were."

"Were you worried?"

"I wanted to talk to you about getting older and thinking back. I think a lot of times people get older and think back about a girl or a boy from their past—*the one who got away.* I wanted to tell you that if you didn't hurry up and get back here, that I would be that girl for you."

Their stomachs touched, then their mouths. They undressed each other. Their movements were fluid, deliberate, almost violent. Pent-up. Henry heard the greatest of ovations as his outsides joined forces with her insides. His peripatetic patterns were over. *Of all the minorities—born into, joined, and otherwise—of all the private clubs and subcultures, love is by far the most exclusive*, he thought. *It's amazing: a one-hundred-ten-pound girl fills immensity.*

She held him, naked. "Much better than make-believe."

"We'll always eat meals together," he said, his hand covering her privates like a leaf. "You and me, no matter what."

Jorden put her thumb in his mouth. "We'll watch bow hunting while we eat."

Just before midnight Henry got out of bed to go to the bathroom. He looked in the mirror as he washed his hands. He looked different, better, as if he was who he was. But the Irukandji looked a little deflated. Henry tapped the Tupperware. He brought it into the bedroom. "Jorden," he whispered. "Jorden." She didn't answer. Very quietly, he bundled up. He decided not to wake her. He decided to go it alone. Before he left, Henry leaned down and whispered in her unpierced ear, "I'd have never let you get away."

It was a quarter-mile walk to the bus stop, and then about twenty minutes to Tenean Beach. It was right in the middle of Dorchester, a predominantly Irish, blue-collar neighborhood, and from the stubby stretch of sand you could see the planes taking off from Logan Airport. Only about a thousand feet wide and bordered by graffitied tenements, industrial warehouses, and the Southeast Expressway, it was said to be a popular spot for gangsters to bury their dead. Henry always thought sunbathing was stupid, but to think that the bathers were lying on corpses made him lie awake at night when he was little.

It was 11:30; Henry walked fast. The bus driver looked at him funny when he boarded. "What's with the fish?" he said.

"It's not a fish," said Henry. "It's a Cnidarian."

The bus dropped him off just before midnight. It was freezing out; the moon looked slightly bronzed, like the Chuck E. Cheese coins. There were no gangsters, no corpses washed up on shore. Sure enough, Old Man Shocket's dinghy was just where Henry remembered it. It had been there for years, tied to a stray piece of concrete. Carved in the side of the boat was a message: FEEL FREE TO USE. FEEL BAD IF YOU STEAL.

Henry untied the boat. The Tupperware fit neatly under the seat. He pulled himself in and shoved off. His father had said that jellies would die if they washed up on shore, so Henry rowed out about sixty feet, and then—*shit!*—he stopped and banged the bottom of the boat. He'd forgotten the stinger suit. As he thought about going back, he looked at the sky and found Polaris. He pictured the stars as glow-in-the-dark stickers. He made a wish and carefully lifted the lid of the Tupperware, leaned on the oar, and spilled the contents into the Atlantic. The Irukandji drifted next to the boat, wagging its tentacles. Henry kept his hands away from the water, doing his best to avoid the fate of the prominent Frenchman.

Tomorrow Henry would go home and talk to his father. There was room for him now. Tomorrow he would buy Jorden a dozen roses. Tomorrow he would—

The oar snapped. Henry fell in, on top of the Irukandji.

His muscles clenched. He never knew water could be so painful. He quickly lost sensation in his toes, then his feet, then his legs. Henry splashed and flailed, flipping the boat, lamely paddling to keep his head above the icy water, holding on to the jelly as if it were a life raft. The insulated stinger suit would have saved him. He could feel the gravity pulling him down as he thought back to the surfing expeditions with his father — how, from the safety of the sofa, Dad would offer his arm: "Grab the log, boy!" he'd yell, his fingers stick-straight and tense. But there was no log, no sofa, no Dad, and minutes later, his body just stopped. There was no more movement, no more air bubbles, and Henry Every slowly slipped from this world into the other.

In the morning, a shell painter found the soggy body washed up on the shore. Henry's lungs had gone salty from the sea, but there was no toxin in his body, no lesions on his face, neck, and forearms. He'd simply drowned. The Irukandji had recognized him from the self-portrait that was taped to the tank.

36

The ants just wouldn't stop crawling. No matter how much luxury was forced upon them, the insects remained as faithful and busy as ever. The contest was just two days away, and the experiment, according to Hannah, was a failure.

"All depends on how you see it," said Harlan. They were eating chocolate fondue with shortbread and strawberries. She liked the shortbread; he liked the strawberries. "All depends on what we were trying to prove."

"Let's go have another look," she said.

"You go," said Harlan, dipping a cookie into the hot pot of chocolate. "I'm gonna clean up."

Hannah walked into the bug room and looked down at her subjects. "What's that?" she said.

"What?" called Harlan.

She was staring at a giant cream-colored insect sitting still in the middle of the terrarium. "What *is* that?" There were ants crawling all over its head and body. "A termite?" She reached in and poked it. She poked again. It wasn't dead. It wasn't even a bug. She shook off the ants and pulled it out for a closer look. It was a box made to look like a giant termite. There was a latch on the back.

Harlan came in from the kitchen. He was wearing his stinger suit.

"Why are you wearing that?"

"I'm sorry for pretending to sleep while you cried. And for trying to be witty, and for making you feel stupid about Galahad, and a whole bunch of other stuff."

"Galahad?"

"It's not important. It's not—"

"The flawless son of Lancelot? The one who gets the girl?"

Harlan beamed. *Girl* instead of *grail*. He unzipped the suit. "Open the latch," he said. "Open it up."

She opened the latch on the box. Inside was a ring. A solid platinum weaver ant with diamonds for eyes.

Her husband knelt down. He was bare-chested, the stinger suit hanging around his waist.

She knelt down in front of him. "We should both kneel," she said.

"I'll carry extra nectar in my belly," he said. "And if you ever get hungry, I promise, I'll throw up in your mouth."

She put the ring on her finger and crawled on top of him. "I'll carry extra nectar, too." She looked up at him, her palms flat against his chest. She pulled the stinger suit down to his ankles. "You won't be needing this anymore."

Winter came early that year. Record low temperatures, but no snow. By New Year's Day, the Every house was almost finished —they'd spent the last six months making it *theirs* again. Hannah had all of her fundamentals sent from the Netherlands, and every room now bore her touches. Henry's old playroom was turned into a study, his ledger bound in leather on an antique chest, his tiny self-portrait framed and hung dead center on the wallpapered wall. There were no tanks, no terrariums — just a man and a woman in a house. Sometimes Hannah would feel trapped and look up at the ceiling, as if maybe she'd catch someone looking down at them.

Harlan had grown a bushy beard. Inspired by Jorden, he had taken to reading *JAMA* and the *DSM-IV*. He was working on being a better engager. Engagers deal with their problems as they come up, he'd learned, as opposed to avoiders, who bury them deep and hope they'll stay buried. Engagers can live happily ever after with other engagers; avoiders can thrive with other avoiders. But when the two mix: trouble.

At 4 A.M. one rainy morning, Harlan woke Hannah. "You shake me off in your sleep," he told her.

"I do?" said Hannah, too tired to comprehend the charge.

"Yes," said Harlan. "When I try to get close you shake me off."

"I'm sorry," she said. "I'm sleeping."

"That's just it," he said. "It feels like a natural response, maybe the most natural."

Hannah threw her leg over his. "I forgive you," she said, and fell back to sleep.

At breakfast the next morning Harlan asked: "What did you mean, 'I forgive you.'"

Hannah put her fork down. She knew he wasn't talking about the previous night. She stalled, fixing on her hard-boiled eggs, then his, scrambled. "It was easier," she said, looking up at the ceiling, remembering the heart-shaped magnet. "It was easier than saying forgive me."

Harlan got up and walked into the study. He sat on the sofa and looked out the window, into the backyard. The driveway was wet, black. Hannah came in and sat down next to him. She looked out the window, too. Harlan turned to

Henry's self-portrait, alone on the wall. He stared at it, studying the features.

"He looks like me, doesn't he?"

Hannah looked at her husband. She looked at their son. "Yes," she said. She couldn't help but notice the resemblance.

"I know the answer! The answer lies within the
heart of all mankind! The answer is twelve?
I think I'm in the wrong building."

— *Charles M. Schulz*

Acknowledgments

Thanks to Leslie Falk — Super Agent, pal — for always know-ing the answer. Heidi Pitlor, editorial alchemist, thanks for inviting me into the right building. This book is because of you both. Mimi and Aunt Evie — for the room, and the lob-ster, and the love. Generous brains: Lisa Ann Gershwin (medusa whiz), Seamus McGraw (woodsman), Dr. Andrew Kapustin and Dr. Ariel Friedman (corporal guides), Larry Rosenbluth (gunman), Andrew Sacher (longtime enabler), Larry Krasner (mailman), and Carl Elliot's edifying *Better Than Well*. Esteemed readers: Sivan Baron, Celine Coudert, Robin Dolch. Jeffrey Mandel, Esquire — for telling me not to write this book. Down-to-business, down-to-earth Sylvie Rabineau, and the A-team at Plan B: Kristin Hahn and Dede Gardner. Gina Kapustin — for your head, bed, heart, and cof-fee. And most of all, thanks to my family, Mom and Dad and Rachel, for saying yes and saying no and saying nothing.